THE PERCEPTIONIST

The Perceptionist

A Novel

MO'REESE MADU

FIRST DECOLONIZED MINDS EDITION,
DECEMBER 2020

Book designed by *Bojan* and *Aallshaa*

ISBN: 978-1-732899377 (paperback)

Printed in the *United States of America*

To Mary, who showed me worlds outside of my own.
To Rai, who saw in me what others missed.
To Ashley, who added to my vision.

ONE

I NEVER BELIEVED IN MESSIAHS, UNTIL A PECULIAR woman appeared in Liberty Heights and showed me otherwise.

Her name was Asè. At least, that's what everyone called her. Not Mrs. or Misses Asè, just the one word, Asè. I didn't know much about her, and neither did anyone else from around here. But she seemed to know everything about us.

She was an elder but had a youthful appearance. Her high-level energy and wrinkle-free skin resembled a woman in her forties. But her ancient demeanor and wisdom confirmed that she was at least in her sixties. She spoke softly but with deep power. And every single time I saw her, she was carrying this old brown leather duffle bag.

I was about twenty-two years old when I first laid eyes on her. She approached my ride, asking to get in, and for some strange reason, I let her. Looking back on that moment, the ancestors must have been guiding me. Any other time, with any other person running up on me the way she did, I would have pulled out my strap and ran them off scared.

I had been sitting in my car, crying, and I guess she heard me. My tears were birthed from a phone call I received that morning, informing me that my best friend Jeremy was found bloody and breathless with two bullet holes in his head.

Although he was only seven years older than me, Jeremy was like my father. My real dad died from cancer ten years earlier. And my mom kicked me out of the house when I was sixteen. So, Jeremy was pretty much the only family I had left.

I spent the rest of that day making calls and visits to folks who knew him, looking for answers to who took 'em out. I spoke with everybody from his mama to his customers but had no luck. After running around all day doing the police's job, I drove down to the old abandoned King Park where me and Jeremy first met to reminisce.

I was riding dirty, so I parked on the opposite side of the gym, underneath the bridge crossing over Harden Street. After turning off my black 88' Cutlass on twenty-twos, I fired up a blunt I had rolled before arriving. No one was usually out this late, especially not here—which is why I was so surprised when I looked up and saw Asè.

"Hey there, son," she said, lightly knocking on my halfway rolled tinted window. "Are you okay?"

Immediately, I dropped the blunt in the ashtray and reached for my Glock 40 under the seat.

"Relax, son. I heard you crying, and I just wanted to

check and see if you were alright."

I wiped my eyes and looked all around my car to see who else was with her. When I didn't see anyone, I became suspicious. The jack boys were always hitting licks, so I felt like this could be a set-up. *Is this lady trying to rob me?*

The old woman placed her hands on her hips. "Do I look like a robber to you?"

I wondered how she knew what I was thinking, but her presence was so engaging; it slipped my mind to ask. "Nah, you don't," I replied with a half smile.

"So, what's wrong, son?"

"Nothing, I'm good."

"Well, you don't look good. Do you want to talk about it?"

"No disrespect, lady, but I don't know you. So there ain't nothing for us to talk about."

"Well, I AM Asè. And you are Dane. Now that we got that out of the way, would you—"

"Hold up," I shouted. "How you know my name?"

"C'mon now," she said. "You know everyone knows you around here."

"True," I replied, nodding, flattered by her comments. "But I ain't never seen you around here before. And whatchu doing out this late … Do you know where you at, lady?"

"I sure do, son. I'm at the *old* King Park. And I came here to see you."

"See me for what? Are you the police, lady?"

"Chile please," the old woman said laughingly. "If I were the police, I would've arrested you on the spot for that unregistered gun in your hand. The blunt in your ashtray. The weed in your glove department. And the rifle in your trunk."

My jaw dropped, stunned at how she knew what I had in my glove department and trunk. "So if you not the popo, then who the hell are you, lady?" I said with my hands raised.

"I told you, son. I'm Asè. Now, if you don't mind, could I have a seat next to you … so we can get started?"

My eyebrows raised with confusion. "Get started doing what?"

Asè glanced down at her duffle bag, then looked back up, peering into my eyes. "We need to start perceiving some things about your life. We need to check out your vision and develop some discernment."

After receiving no response, the old woman asked, "So… can we continue this convo inside or you gon keep an old lady out here in the cold?"

I was skeptical as hell about this lady. I didn't know who she was or where she came from. But there was something about her boldness that put me at ease. Any woman with the guts to come out here this late at night by herself was an OG in my book, which earned my respect. Plus, I was curious about what she wanted to discuss.

"Yeah, you can come in."

"Thanks, son." Looking down into my window, she said, "You know, you can take your fingers off that trigger now? I promise I won't rob you." She grinned.

"Oh, my bad, I forgot about that," I said, as I slowly

placed the gun back underneath my seat.

I watched the old woman closely as she walked around to the passenger side, noticing that she was carrying an old brown leather handbag on her shoulder. This made me even more suspicious of her intentions, but when she opened the door and sat down, her aura prompted me to relax.

Asè was a beautiful old lady. She had glowing caramel skin, beautiful long dreadlocks hanging over her shoulders, and a smile bright as the sun. She wore a regal African dress, which covered her from shoulder to ankle, only allowing her feet to be seen inside her leather sandals. And her aroma, which smelled like lavender and roses, filled the car like brand new air freshener.

She was also dripped in solid gold. Her loop earrings matched the ankh on her ring finger, the birthstone plates on her pinky finger, and the triangular gemstones around her neck and wrists. I had never met a woman with a presence like hers before. She looked like royalty, yet was ever so humble. And her calming, familiar smile had me mesmerized. *Who is this lady?*

"I'm Asè, remember?" she asked with a slight grin.

"Huh? I didn't say nothing."

"Yes you did," she responded. "You just didn't open your mouth."

My eyes grew as wide as the moon. "So you can read people's minds, lady?"

"Oh no, I don't have that gift, honey," she answered. "I'm just a Perceptionist."

"A what?"

"A Perceptionist," she repeated. "I perceive things about life that other people miss. Things that produce change but are hidden behind obstacles." The old lady tilted her head toward the full moon behind the oak trees. "I see conditions and circumstances with full discernment. And that's all most people lack—is discernment—seeing the truth of a matter. So I hold the mirror up for 'em … and it empowers them to pause, gain clarity, and transform their lives for the better."

After a short staring contest between me and the old lady, I picked up my blunt from the ashtray and began lighting it up. "I see this is going to be a long night. You don't mind, do you?"

"It's your ride, son. I'm just a guest. Besides, the herbs may help you better interpret what you're going to learn tonight. Just don't blow it my way, okay?" she said sternly.

"Bet."

For a few minutes, we sat quietly, peering off at the moon and the stars covering the sky. I was strangely at ease in the presence of this mysterious woman, who was now comfortably reclined on the headrest. As I blew my last puff out of my window, Asè gently touched me on my shoulder. "So … your best friend passed on, huh?"

My head turned so fast my neck could've snapped. "What the hell … How you know that lady?"

She shrugged her shoulders. "Word travels fast around here, son."

"Yeah, but you don't live out here. So how did it get to

you?"

"Boy, you a sharp one, ain't ya," she grinned. "I've been in and out of Columbia since before you were born. But you can check my credentials out later, chile. Right now, I just want you to know that I am sorry for your loss ... but if you don't make some serious changes in your life, you gon end up just like your friend."

"So, you came here to tell me I'm going to die?"

"No, you already know that," she said. "We're all going to die one day. But death is a matter of discernment too." My face followed my mind, looking at this lady like she was crazy. "The flesh is temporary, but the spirit is eternal."

"I don't know about that spiritual stuff, ma'am. But I'm in the flesh, and Jeremy ain't. So If I'm alive, then he's dead."

Carefully, Asè asked, "Well, why do you think that is? Why do you think you lived, and Jeremy didn't?"

"It's my fault. But it's a long story."

"Well, I ain't got nothing but time, son. So tell me ... why do you blame yourself for the death of your friend?"

I took a deep breath and sighed. "Because he went on a dope run for me in my place. Normally, I make that run, but this time he did it for me."

Suddenly, my mind went into overdrive, replaying the last conversation I had with Jeremy. It had been two days since we last talked, just before I sent him on a run to sell a quarter kilo of cocaine to some out-of-towners. Guilt seeped into every fiber, bone, and muscle in my body. *I should have been dead, not Jeremy*, I thought to myself. But Asè interrupted my guilt trip.

"Do you think that was a coincidence?" she asked. "I mean, out of all your runs, do you think it's a coincidence that this one particular time he goes, and you don't … you live and he doesn't?"

"Lady, I don't know. Is this your way of trying to convince me that it ain't my fault?"

"No," the old lady said calmly. "I just wanted to see what level of discernment you had."

"Oh. Well, I grew up hearing all that discernment talk about faith and God choosing who he wants to live and die. But I don't believe in religion if that's where you're headed."

"Oh no, son. I don't believe in religion either. And I'm not here to convert you to anything."

Noticing the vexed expression on my face, Asè became quiet, gathering her thoughts, it seemed. Then she glanced over at me with her angelic eyes and smiled. "Dane, what would you say if I told you that Jeremy was going to end up dead that night regardless—but as a result of his death, you are exactly where you need to be, to create the life you desire to live?"

"I would say, how do you know that?"

"Because I've been watching Jeremy too. And the choices he made landed him where he's at."

"So how come you ain't try to stop him from being killed then?" I yelled. "He was my best friend."

"I can't stop anyone from doing anything, son. All I can do is offer discernment." She exhaled before adding, "But it was too late for Jeremy. His karma reached him before I did."

I stared at the old lady for several seconds in a daze about what she just said. "So, what did you mean earlier about me being exactly where I needed to be?"

"Well, this is your chance to remember who you are … before it's too late."

"And who is that?"

"You tell me," she said with her hands on her hips. "Or better yet. What is it that you've been staying up late doing ever since you were a lil boy?"

"Writing movies," I answered quickly. "Wait. How did you know—" I shook my head. "Never mind."

Asè giggled.

"Yes. You're a writer," she said. "That is your gift to the world. You were sent here to uplift your people through the power of stories. But like many folks around here in the 'Heights,' you have lost your way. So, now is the perfect time for you to get back on the path of your destiny."

I sat quietly for a few moments, just pondering her words. The old woman had lit a fire of possibility in me that I didn't want to be put out. Then, in the back of my mind, "But how do I even start a writing career?" I asked. "All I know is the streets … and selling dope."

Asè smiled at me with pure compassion and said, "In order to accomplish the work you were created to do, you have to become the person you were created to be." She saw the strange look on my face and decided to explain further.

"You see, many people want to be writers, son. Just

like many people want to be athletes and entrepreneurs. But if you notice, in each of those fields, only a *few* are successful, right?"

I nodded.

"Well, that's because the majority of people are not willing to let go of the people, places, and habits that are contrary to their goals. Like sheep, they fear being separated from the flock, which causes them to remain where they are," she said staring to my eyes. "But every now and then, one from the pack decides it's time for a change—often after reaching the lowest point in their life—and they too, go on to become one of the *few*."

"So, as I mentioned earlier, you're exactly where you need to be." The old woman glanced around the parking lot and spotted a rose growing from the concrete. "You see that rose right there?" she pointed. "That's you, son—surrounded by hardships. And once you commit to your calling, you will rise above your environment."

Before she left that night, Asè opened her duffle bag, holding it carefully away from my view, and removed three books from it. "Do you read, son?"

"Nah, not really. I ain't read a book since middle school," I laughed with pride as if it was a badge of honor not to read. With a straight face, she replied, "Well, if you're going to be a writer, you will have to become a reader. So read these."

I looked at the books she handed me in the light from my car. They were all written by black authors. The titles were: *The Autobiography of Malcolm X*, *How to Get Out of Your Own*

Way, and *Oscar Micheaux*.

"Are all these biographies?" I asked.

"Even better," she said. "These are the *eyes* of great black men who have risen out of the slums like you. It includes their successes, failures, lessons, and wisdom. By reading the wisdom of these great men, you will discover what made them great . . . which will give you the discernment to become great yourself."

Then Asè looked down inside the small opening of her bag and smiled. I didn't know what she was smiling at, but it made me smile in return. "Well, that's my time, son. It's getting late. I should be getting home now."

"Wait, let me give you a ride."

"Thanks, son. But I prefer to walk."

I begged her to let me take her home to make sure she was safe, but she insisted that she was 'safer than I was on these streets' and that she needed the exercise. So we laughed and said our goodbyes. I stayed in the parking lot for a while, meditating on all the gems she dropped. I felt ashamed for not being nicer to the old lady, especially since I was no longer devoid of hope as I had been before she arrived.

AFTER ABOUT AN HOUR OR SO, I RUSHED HOME to my apartment and began reading my new books. The first one I picked up was, *How to Get Out of Your Own Way* by Tyrese Gibson. The book was so good, it kept me up all night. It was inspiring to learn that he grew up in the hood, just like me, and made it out to become a worldwide star.

The following day, I went to Jeremy's wake with my homies. While waiting for the doors to open, I ran into the funeral director, Mr. Reed, who buried my Father. He asked me how I knew Jeremy, so I told him the truth, and after a brief small talk, I discovered that he also knew Asè. "Yeah, man, she's the one who inspired me to get into the funeral business back in the day," he said. "Before that, I was a knucklehead, just like you."

He proceeded to tell me that he'd seen her around recently and that she looked the exact same as she did thirty years ago. *He must be exaggerating,* I thought.

THAT NIGHT I BEGAN READING *The Auto-Biography of Malcolm X*. I knew very little about him, so I was surprised to learn that he came from the same world of selling drugs as me. Although I had no interest in converting to Islam, the way it radically transformed his life was very inspiring. And the messages he preached convinced me to leave the streets behind.

By the next morning, I had completed the book, walking away from it a different person than I was before reading it. I sold my last ounce of dope later that afternoon and combined it with my re-up money to pay back my plug for the work I gave to Jeremy. When I told 'em I was done, he tried to convince me otherwise, but my mind was made up!

Before I went to bed that night, I read *Oscar Micheaux*. I never heard of him before, but his life turned out to be just as interesting as the others. Learning about how he grew up as the son of slaves and yet went on to become the first black filmmaker in America, motivated me even more to pursue my dream.

As soon as I finished reading, I thought about Asè. I was anxious as hell to share with her all the gems I was picking up from those books. But it would be a few more days before I saw her again.

TWO

I WAS SHOOTING POOL AT GILLIAN'S; GAMBLING to make up for all the money I was losing not being in the streets. After Tony shot the last hole in the left corner pocket to barely win against me, the old woman slipped up behind me. "How's it going, son?"

I was highly upset at my loss because I desperately needed that money. But after seeing Asè, I immediately perked up.

"Hey Asè!" I exclaimed. "I didn't see you come in. Way you been? I've been looking for you. I read all the books!" While my homies and the rest of the fellas around my area were looking at me weirdly, Asè chuckled at my enthusiasm; and the lack thereof around me.

"Slow down, son. Let me talk back. The night ain't going nowhere," she grinned. "And chile you look so nervous, you wouldn't have seen me if I wasn't sitting on the table."

Tony laughed as he gathered my money from the chair and walked away.

"I've been around though," she finally answered. "I even passed by you a few times—I just didn't wanna bother ya. But I'm glad you read the books. Did you learn anything?"

"Did I?" My head tilted backward. "I learned so much, I don't know where to start. It's like a whole new world has opened up to me."

"That's good to hear, son. So which one was your favorite?" The old woman asked as we headed towards the exit.

"The Autobiography of Malcolm X!" I exclaimed. "I couldn't put it down—I highlighted almost the whole book."

"Yeah," she smiled, "I figured you would enjoy Malcolm's story. Y'all have a lot in common."

"Yeah, right!" I laughed.

"I'm for real, son. The same greatness in him lives in you."

After exiting the pool hall, we walked toward the rowdy streets in front of the plaza. Asè pulled out two brown paper bags from her duffle bag and extended one towards me. "You hungry?"

"Hell yeah ... I meant yes ma'am."

She laughed. "Well, c'mon, let's sit down. I got some good ol' soul food for us." The "soul food" turned out to be a steamed veggie avocado bowl. I was disappointed in her food selection—and she knew it—but I was hungry, so I ate.

We sat on a bench in front of the Palmetto Lake walkway across the street from the plaza. The state fair was in town this week, so almost the entire community was out this night. Parents were playing with their children behind us and the calming blue waters in front of us.

"So, what you grubbing on, son?" Asè asked me, peering into me with a gentle smile.

I looked at her, clueless. "What you talking 'bout Asè?" I said while wiping my mouth from the sauce on my fork. "I'm eating the same thing you eating."

"You think so?" the old lady teased.

"Oh, I forgot who I'm talking to," I grinned. "So what do you perceive I'm eating Asè?"

She leaned over, glancing at my food. "You tell me, son?" Seeing the wheels spinning in my head for answers, Asè responded compassionately. "It's not a trick question son."

I shrugged my shoulders. "Well, I guess I'm —."

"Ah-ah. No guessing son. Just tell me what you're eating."

"Okay. I'm eating an avocado bowl. Just yummy," I said sarcastically.

Playfully shaking her head, she asked, "And where are you eating it at?"

I was stilled puzzled. But I decided to go along. "Outside. On a bench."

Asè smiled. "Well, the books are helping with knowledge," she said. "But I will have to help you with your sight."

"What are you talking about now Asè?"

"Your perception son … It's still foggy. But I'm sure we can clean out that pineal gland of yours and expand our view."

I gave her a look of frustration. "I don't even know what a pineal gland is … or what that has to do with what I'm eating."

Asè laughed out loud, then scooted over and placed her hand on my shoulder. "I know you don't son. But you will by the end of tonight."

The old woman then released her arm from my shoulder and raised her finger with authority. "Here is a universal law for ya ... one that will change your entire life if you grasp it." As I leaned forward with anticipation, she declared, "Whatever you focus on, grows. And whatever you ignore, dies."

I frowned, trying to understand this new riddle of hers. Thankfully she didn't leave me hanging.

"It means," she went on to explain, "when you focus your mind on things that you *don't* have, you'll discover more and more things you lack—things that you probably forgotten about—and you will feel even worse. On the other hand," she said "when you focus on what you *do* have and are grateful for it, you'll receive more to be grateful for."

I was much less enthusiastic about her wisdom this second time around. Perceiving this, she put her food aside and shifted her body to face me directly. "Let's try it this way son. When you were at the pool hall hustling tonight, what was your focus?"

After a quick thought, I said, "Winning the game."

"*Chile* please. If that was truly your focus, then you would have won. Aren't you one of the best pool players around here?"

I wondered how she knew that. "Yes ma'am!"

"And haven't you beat Tony many times before?"

"All the time. I can't believe he beat me tonight. I was so

pissed."

"So what was different about tonight ... what were you focusing on during the game?"

"I guess I was—"

"No, don't guess son. Tell me what you know!"

"Ok," I said. "I was focusing on not losing the game."

"Bingo!" she grinned. "You see that? By focusing on what you didn't want ... losing grew from being just a thought to a reality."

My jaw dropped almost to the floor. "WOW! That's deep Asè," I said. "I get what you saying now."

"Good, I was beginning to wonder about you." She bumped me on the shoulder and laughed. But I was too busy processing her words to laugh back.

"So if I had focused on winning like I normally do ... then I probably would have won right?" I asked excitedly.

"You got it, son!" The old woman beamed at my enthusiasm. "But let's dive a little deeper. Tell me this: What was it that made you so desperate to win that game?"

"Well since I took your advice and gave up dealing drugs," I said sarcastically, "I've been a lil short on funds. I mean I ain't broke, but I got bills to pay. So I really needed that money."

"Hmm ... So you were focusing on *lack* in this situation too, huh?"

"Yeah," I said, narrowing my eyes. "But my money was getting short so there wasn't nothing else for me to focus on."

"That's not true son," she proclaimed. "You don't lack

money, you lack discernment. There is opportunity all around you to earn money … doing exactly what you love."

"Like where?"

"Well let me ask you this, son. Where do opportunities come from—people or places?"

Here she goes again. "People," I answered.

"That's right," she said. "And what makes a person give someone else an opportunity?" I tried to think of an answer, but nothing came. "Well, when you were out there slanging in the streets all these years, what type of people did you let move drugs for you?"

"Hustlers," I answered. "Niggas that know how to make money."

She shook her head at my use of the n-word and then continued. "So … people you could *trust* to deliver … right?"

"Yes ma'am."

"And how did you *know* these people?"

"From the streets. We either grew up together or I met 'em from my homies."

"So … people you had a relationship with, right?"

"Uh-huh!"

"Did you *like* everybody who sold for you?"

"For sho!" I nodded. "We like brothers. Or at least we were."

"Well son," she said like a proud mother, "you just explained to me the law of compensation." I scratched my head as she continued. "In so many words, you told me that you gave people opportunities based on three pillars: knowing them, liking them, and trusting them."

"This is also how the gatekeepers for most businesses and companies think. They grant people opportunities based on the same criteria." She waved at a couple who greeted her in passing and then returned her attention to me. "So," she said cheerfully, "since opportunities come from people, what happens to a person who everyone knows, likes, and trusts in their industry?"

I was beginning to catch on. "They get more opportunities?"

"Bingo," Asè affirmed. "And when your life is filled with opportunities, you will always be successful."

I beamed at the possibility of a successful life.

Noticing the fresh hope and excitement on my face, Asè held up her index finger and added, "But I must warn you, son. All universal laws work in dualities. So when a person is not known, liked or trusted—they won't get many, if any opportunities at all—no matter how gifted they are. And we all know what happens to people with a lack of opportunities … right?"

The old woman turned around glancing at a group of homeless by the gate begging folks for money. After turning around to peep the scenery myself, I answered, "Things get worse and worse and they end up stuck in the *mud*."

Asè paused for a moment to let the truth of my statement sink in. Looking her dead in the eyes, I said, "So how can I become a person that the movie industry folks know, like, and trust?"

"Good question son." She pondered for a second. "Try this out. Every day you wake up to accomplish your dreams, ask yourself this: Does my character line up with my goals?"

"Ok. But why that question?"

"Because your character must be in alignment with what you desire to manifest," she answered. "So if your lifestyle—meaning the actions you take on a day to day basis and the people you spend the most time around—is out of sync with being a movie writer, then you won't attract those in the industry to you."

"Dang," I said with my bottom lip poked out. "I *see* I have a lot to work on."

"Aww don't be down son. *Seeing* is a good thing. You can't change what you can't see. That's why I'm here … to help you see."

For the next half hour, we both sat silently watching the ducks in the river, listening to playful conversations of parents having just as much fun as their children. Then Asè got up to gather our food baskets and placed them in the trash. Walking back, she extended her hand motioning for me to get up. "Tonight you ate an avocado bowl on a city bench," she said amusingly. "But I dined on Mother Nature's finest with a lakeside view and the spirit of love and laughter all around me." She patted me on the back. "Life is all about perception."

We walked to the plaza where my car was parked. Before departing, she pulled out three more books from her bag, in exchange for the last ones she gave me; which I left in my car in case I ran into her again. "Thanks, Asè. I really appreciate it."

"You're welcome, son. I'm getting them from Baba's." She pointed toward what looked like a bookstore. "They have the best selections of books on our people, and I've been picking them out specifically for you." As she attempted to drift off, I grabbed her arm.

"Asè, for once would you please let me give you a ride home?" I asked. "I mean, that's the least I can do," I said with my hands raised.

"I'm already home son," she said with an angelic-like smile. Then she waved her hand back and forth. "Now get. You got books to read."

I watched her walk off into the sunset, on another mission I assumed, and then I drove off.

SHE HAD LEFT ME DOZENS OF BOOKS DURING my few short months of knowing her. And though it was so long ago, I can still remember all of them.

The next three books she gave me were titled: *Marcus Garvey*, *Booker T. Washington and Africa*, and *Makes Me Wanna Hollar*. Then it was *Hubert Harrison*, *Empire*, and *The Secret to Success*. And then finally I was given *Green Power*, *John Henrick Clarke*, and *The Autobiography of Leroi Jones*. Hidden in the back of the last one was a note from Asè, instructing me to return these books to Baba's. So I did.

Baba's was the only blacked-owned bookstore in town. It was part-library as well; which is mostly what kept it open. While I was there returning and checking out more books, the store owner Baba Kambon told me that our mutual friend informed him that I was a writer and that he was looking to hire someone who could write short stories for his weekly newsletters. I gladly accepted, and though I was rusty, my first few issues were a big hit.

Within a few weeks, I noticed that Asè had left. I looked for her everywhere, but she was ghost. Yet, I found traces of her deeds at almost every turn.

Asè had arranged for Ella, the owner of The Soul Hub, a restaurant in Liberty Plaza, to hire me as a freelance content writer for their print and online marketing promotions. My natural ability to hustle led to a major increase in sales, which caused Ella also to give me 20% commissions on every customer that came from my marketing efforts.

Soon, more and more local businesses started hiring me as a content writer on a freelance basis, and in some cases, I got to write the scripts for online and TV commercials; which gave me a foot in the door of my dreams. And every single time, without fail, Asè's name was mentioned. So although I didn't see her, I knew she had "been around."

THE NEXT FEW YEARS FLEW BY LIKE THE WIND. I continued reading biographies but after noticing how much racially-motivated obstacles our people had to endure to become successful, I began to read other books as well— on history, systematic racism, social psychology, etc.—to gain an understanding of the causes behind our plight. In doing so, I realized the majority of our issues were due to a lack of unity and ownership. So I began to theme my writing around those issues, and locally, became known as the voice of the people.

After freelancing around town for a few years, I was offered a screenwriting gig for a black TV show in LA. I took it, and in less than a year, I was able to purchase my first house. That show was canceled after the second season, but that gig led to another, which led to another, and I eventually became one of the most sought-after pro-black writers in Hollywood.

However, I knew that ownership was the key to controlling my destiny. So, about five years ago, I started my own production company, called 'Our Stories Entertainment.' My first movie, *It Takes A Village*, was a box office hit and has since been screened internationally. It is now used by teachers, professors, activists, and organizations, as a teaching tool for instilling love and unity within the black family.

Even to this day, I find myself blown away by the responses to that film.

DURING THE Q&A PORTION OF A LECTURE I DID at Howard University a few months ago, a student asked me a question that took me back to where it all started.

"Mr. Carter, your film has changed my life. The way I view the world, the way I view myself, the way I interact with our people … hell, the way I do everything," the young man said, laughingly. "My question for you is … How did you come up with the principles in this story?"

"I guess you could say—" I stopped myself, still hearing Asè's voice in my head after all these years, saying, *no guessing son.*

"Well, the truth is … when I was young, I crossed paths with this sweet old lady by the name of Asè, who taught me the principles that I showcased in this movie. And … these principles helped me become the man I am today. So had it not been for Asè, I probably wouldn't even be alive, let alone writing movies."

"Ohhh. Ok." He nodded. "So this is where the phrase Asè came from, that you use in the movie?"

"Nah not really," I said. "Asè is a West African word from the Yoruba people. It means 'the power and authority to make whatever you say happen.' And it's often said at the end of an empowering quote or prayer. You know … like how Christians say Amen … but this phrase works." I laughed out loud.

"Ahh-shay," the students in the front rows shouted in unison like a church choir. I smiled, flattered at the students' use of the word.

"Yeah," I continued, "So the reason I used the word Asè in the film was mostly for cultural reasons. However, I also wanted to pay homage to the real Asè. The sweet old lady who set me on the right path."

"Well, who is this *real* Asè, Mr. C?" The young man asked. "Is she still alive today?"

"Yeah, Mr. C," another student from the audience yelled out. "Is she still around?"

"Honestly, I don't know. Your guess is as good as mines."

I have thought about Asè every day of my life for the past decade. When I moved to Hollywood, I had wanted her to be at my going-away party. On the day I got married, I scanned the pews the entire service, hoping she would show. After each of our two kid's home-births, I went outside and sat in my car with tears of nervousness about fatherhood, wishing she'd knock on my window and advise me. I would have done just about anything to spend one more day with her. But I never saw Asè again.

Until last month.

THREE

A FEW YEARS AGO I CAME TO THE CONCLUSION that Asè was dead. I didn't have any evidence or clues to back my theory up. Nor did I fully believe it myself. But it was the only way I knew how to be at peace with never seeing her again. So I ran with it.

But then, last month on a Saturday afternoon, I was at the Vegan Soul Bar—it used to be called The Soul Hub when I was younger —the same spot I used to write content for. It's still owned by Ella and my favorite spot to eat at during the summers I'm in town from LA. I was eating a veggie wrap at the bar, chatting with my wife Lashonda when Ella walked over. "Hey Mrs. Ella, how you been?" I said.

"Hey sweetie I can't complain," she answered. "How about you, movie star?"

"Cut it out. I write movies, I don't play in them."

Ella shrugged her shoulders. "Well, you the only person we know around here who made it to Hollywood so you're a star in my book." I smiled.

"So business is still booming I see," Lashonda said, observing the long line at the register.

"Yeah girl," Ella replied cheerfully. "It's been a packed house ever since we re-opened. Faces I ain't seen in years been coming through to support whether they vegan or not."

She was right. There was not one empty seat in the building. But I wasn't surprised because summers in Liberty Heights was like Christmas; it brought in people from all over the state. And this was the hottest restaurant in town.

"It's been good seeing your old friend back around here too," Ella said, smiling. "I missed her so much."

"Old friend?" I asked. "Who you talking about Ella?"

"Yeah. Who is she?" My wife demanded.

"Whoa. Calm down," Ella answered. "I'm talking about Asè." She pointed somewhere behind me. "She came in a few minutes ago with Pastor Smalls' wife." Ella saw the shock on my face as I quickly turned around to scope out the restaurant. "Oh my bad, I thought you knew she was back."

I detected her at the left corner table by the window. Although her back was to the door, her old brown leather duffle bag sitting on the table, gave her away. I was so excited, I almost peed in my pants.

"How long has she been back," I asked Ella.

"Maybe a few months now," she said. "But she looks like she never left."

She did look the same. Her hair was still beautifully locked, a little longer perhaps, but not much. The dress she had on looked like one I had seen her in years ago. And the gold jewelry on her neck and fingers still glistened like the sun.

I got up and paced between the tables, moving slowly towards the right of Asè. Kevin and Tina Smalls, the pastors of the church that my mother attended, spotted me first, and Kevin waved his hand and nodded. It was obvious I was headed towards their table, so I guess he assumed I wanted to talk to them; even though we hadn't spoken in years.

My hands dripped with sweat as I approached their table. "Asè!" I shouted, probably a little too loud. She turned around and smiled so widely that I could see all of her teeth. "WOW!" I said, leaning in to tackle her with a bear hug. "It's really you. I thought you were dead. Where have you been all these years? I wanted to tell you I made it!"

"I know, I know," she said as she got up to embrace me. "It's good to see ya too, son. But slow down … we have plenty of time to catch up."

I must admit I became a little upset. *After 10 years, this is all you have to say to me?* Then I quickly realized that almost the entire restaurant was staring our way trying to see what all the commotion was about—including the Smalls.

"Well hey Dane," Tina said, demandingly.

"Oh. Hey Mrs. Smalls."

"So … how do you two know each other?" she asked.

"It's a long story. But Asè helped me—"

"I met Dane back in the day when he was trying to figure out his way," Asè cheerfully interrupted. Then she looked me up and down checking out my physique. "You ain't all skin and bones no more are you?" she laughed.

"No ma'am. I'm grown now."

"I see," she replied. "Eating good huh?"

"Yep. Mother nature's finest."

"My man," she said with a twinkle in her eyes. Then she grabbed me by the hand and asked "Will you be free later on?"

I looked up and noticed the uncomfortable face on Kevin and felt that I had interrupted an important conversation. "Yeah, why what's up?"

"Well, I want to finish chatting with my new buddies for a few. So how about you meet me down at Baba's in a couple of hours, but in the café, okay?" She smiled and winked. Baba's had expanded some years back as a result of my marketing efforts, and was now called Baba's Books & Cafe.

"Ok. See you in a few hours," I answered.

As I greeted the Smalls goodbye, I couldn't help but notice how upset and confused they looked. I wondered what Asè meant by them being her new buddies.

ABOUT A WEEK EARLIER, PASTOR KEVIN SMALLS had publicly announced that he was no longer a Christian and would be teaching a more empowering message from here on out. In response, his wife, Tina had asked for a divorce after twenty-one years of marriage. She still loved him; she just refused to be yoked to an unbeliever. I ain't going to hell for nobody, she had said.

Kevin had been the pastor at 'Living Through The Word Ministries' for over seventeen years and was a member of the same church for over twenty-three years. He was a devout, pro-black Christian who had never questioned his faith until a few months ago at a community meeting when he overheard an old woman say that gospels of Christ derived from the story of Horus.

Kevin had no idea who *Horus* was so he wasn't sure if he had heard correctly. Walking over to the group of people whom she was talking to, he interrupted her speech and said, "Hey, excuse me ma'am … but what did you say?"

"About what son?" The old woman asked nicely.

"Well, you said something about the original Christ being Horus?"

"Yes. Horus of Ancient Egypt," she replied.

He continued with a few more questions but still was lost. Feeling embarrassed that the younger crowd of men knew more than him, he stopped asking questions and rebuked the old woman. The fellas tried to calm him down, but he quoted scriptures condemning them all. "You are the Devil," he told the old woman as he stormed out of the meeting.

While there, he discovered a book titled, *Christianity Before Christ*, which detailed the origins of the bible. After reading that and a dozen other history books over the next few weeks, Pastor Smalls began to see that Christianity was not as original as he thought.

Kevin tried to convince Tina of the same, but she refused

to entertain him. Instead, she tried to win him back to the faith. After months of arguing with no resolve, Tina served him with papers. Kevin couldn't believe it.

IT WAS ALMOST NOON AND TINA WAS RUSHING out of a women's conference at the church. She was late for a lunch meeting with her husband Kevin; to discuss how the church would be run after their divorce. Tears fell down her cheeks like waterfalls as she got to the exit. Tina loved her husband to death but felt obligated to Christ not to be unequally yoked.

As she was approaching her car in the 'pastors only' section of the parking lot, she heard a greeting from an old lady walking down the street sidewalk. "Hey Mrs. Smalls, how you doing?"

"Hey there," she said without looking up to see who it was. "I'm blessed. How about you?"

"I'm great honey. Thanks for asking." The voice didn't sound familiar, so she glanced in the lady's direction to see who it was, as she put her belongings in the car.

It was Asè. Tina had never seen her before, but she knew quite a few people who had; especially her husband. And the old woman's divine presence confirmed each of their testimonies. *Oh my God. I can't believe it's her.* Tina stood frozen as if she had seen a ghost.

"Are you alright Mrs. Smalls?" asked Asè, walking towards her car.

"Yes ma'am," Tina said, snapping out of it. "I'm just in a hurry to be somewhere."

"Oh ok. Well, I don't want to hold you up. Where ya headed this fine Saturday afternoon? If you don't mind me asking."

"Uh … I was about to go get something to eat," Tina answered.

"Me, too," Asè replied. "I'm meeting an old friend in Liberty Heights. Would you mind giving me a lift?"

She stood silent, contemplating if this was a good idea or not. *So this is the lady that led my husband astray? And she got the audacity to ask me for a ride. This must be a test Lord … Ok. Ok. Get yourself together girl. Let her in.*

"Sure, ma'am. Hop in." Tina motioned for her to open the door on the passenger side.

"Thank ya, Mrs. Smalls. I guess respect for one's elders is not dead, after all, huh?"

"No ma'am. At least not here at the House of the Lord," Tina said, as she closed her door. "But you certainly don't look like an elder. You look younger than me … Miss Asè, is it?"

"No misses, just Asè." The old woman quickly hopped in the passenger side. "But thank you, sweetie. I appreciate the kind words."

Suddenly, the vibration of love filled the car and Tina felt at ease. She cranked up the car and began to head down Main Street towards Liberty Heights. "So, which restaurant you headed to, Asè?"

"The Vegan Soul Bar."

"Really? I'm headed there too."

"I know you are," Asè said with a bright smile. "That's why I asked you for a lift."

Tina turned towards the old woman with her eyebrows raised. "But I thought you said you were meeting an old friend for lunch?"

"I am. My old friend is your husband, Pastor Smalls."

"What?" Tina's eyes tightened with fury. "Kevin invited you to lunch with us?"

Asè placed her hand on Tina's shoulder. "Relax honey. Everything is fine. I'm just here to help."

Tina kept silent the rest of the ride, not even looking in the direction of Asè. As she pulled into the parking lot, she noticed Kevin's tan and chrome Buick. *What is Kevin up to? How could this old woman be Kevin's friend? And why would he invite her to lunch with us … especially on a day like this!*

Pastor Smalls was sitting at the back left corner table looking at his watch when Tina and Asè walked in. When he looked up and saw the two approaching his table, he became nervous. *Who is that with Tina?* He wondered. *OH MY GOD. Is that the old woman from that meeting months ago? I cannot believe she brought her here. What is this about?*

Kevin stood up as the two arrived at the table, saying hey to Tina, and nodding at the old woman. "Hey Kev, long time no see, huh son?" Asè reached for a hug. He returned the hug out of respect but had a confused look on his face. As did Tina!

Then the three sat down and shortly placed their orders. Asè had a salad and a fruit juice and the Smalls had vegan burgers, sweet potato fries, and iced tea. The old woman sat quietly enjoying her food, happy and calm as always. Kevin and Tina, on the other hand, seemed like they were about to explode. They tried to keep their cool by making small talk, each waiting for the other to explain why Asè was there, but the heat was rising all over their faces.

To make things even hotter, they were interrupted for a few minutes by someone—me—who knew each of them. And the fact that they hadn't seen him since he was a teen, yet he somehow knew the old woman, only made them more confused. So after their mutual friend had left, Kevin decided to end the suspense.

He looked to the right at Tina and then across from him at Asè, and said, "Ok. Now I don't mean to be rude ladies, but what the hell is going on?"

Tina quickly turned towards Kevin rolling her eyes. "Excuse me? I should be asking you that. You the one who invited her."

"Huh?" Kevin said, raising his right hand in confusion and anger. "What you talking about? I haven't spoken to this lady in months … since that night at the meeting I told you about."

Tina looked at Asè, waiting for an answer. "He's right Tina. I haven't spoken to Kevin here in almost three months," the old woman said, calmly.

"What? But you told me in the car that he invited you here?"

"No, I didn't honey. Those were your words, not mines."

Tina looked like she was about to hop across the table. Just before she could get the curse words from her mouth, Asè interrupted. "All I said was that I was coming here to meet an old friend. And that Kevin was my friend." Tina thought about it for a moment and realized that the old woman was right.

"But why would you say that we were friends when we don't even know each other?" Kevin asked annoyingly.

"Mm-hmm," Tina responded loudly with her arms folded.

The old woman pushed her plate aside and placed her hands together gently on the table. Looking at Kevin, she said, "Didn't the man you've been preaching about all these years, consider himself a friend to all … even those who hated him?" He nodded. "Well, then how come you find it so irritating that little ol' me would consider you as my friend … even after you called me the Devil?" she grinned.

Kevin looked down, feeling ashamed. "Yeah. About that night. I am so sorry for—"

"I know son," Asè interrupted. "All is forgiven."

The riddles of the old woman had stumped both Kevin and Tina. They each sat there dumbfounded watching her finish her juice. Then Tina, the skeptical one, came to her senses. "Jesus also told everyone the truth," she rebutted. "So if you're our friend, then tell us why we are here mam?"

"To learn and to grow," Asè replied. "Together as one."

"Uhhh," Kevin chimed in. "I think it might be a little too late for—"

"Wait." Tina placed her hand on top of his. "Let the lady

talk." Kevin's eyebrows raised with surprise.

"May I proceed Pastor?" Asè asked gently. Kevin waved his right palm upward, motioning for her to continue.

"So," she said, "Are you two thinking about getting a divorce?"

Kevin's mouth dropped wide open. Tina's eyes widened with shock. "How did you know that Asè?" Tina asked.

"Yeah. How did you?" Kevin added.

The old woman held her hands up. "Easy. Easy. I was just asking y'all a question," she said, grinning. "But from your answer, I can see that it's true."

Tina and Kevin looked at each other, neither knowing what to say. The old woman's answer was so clever and yet so accurate, that it left them stumped.

Then suddenly, Kevin laughed out loud, joining Asè in her delight. "Ok, it's true," he said. "We are in the process of getting a divorce. Now what?"

"Well, before we can get to the 'what', I first need to know the 'why'." Kevin stopped laughing as Asè continued. "So why are you two considering a divorce … Now … after all these years?"

"Because of you," Tina shouted. "Everything was fine until you came along and planted all that African stuff inside Kevin's mind. Now he's lost and on his way to hell."

"See. There you go again with that foolishness Tina. Ain't nobody lost except you?"

"Lost?" Tina yelled. "Negro, I'm saved, sanctified, and filled with the Holy Ghost. You the one that's put your hand to plow and looked back."

Kevin shook his head, and then looked at Asè. "You see what I have to deal with?"

"Well, you guys are definitely married … cuz only married folks argue like this," the old woman said grinning. She then leaned forward as if she was telling them a secret. "But if you wanna stay married, this isn't the way to go about it."

Tina and Kevin kept silent, eager to hear what the old woman had to say next.

"Now that it's clear what you two are at odds about, let's get started," Asè said. "As y'all already know, the divorce rate in America is through the roof, especially among our people. And that is due to a lack of discernment about what marriage actually is."

Discernment? What could you possibly know about that? Tina thought to herself.

Asè smiled at her with compassion and then continued. "Like most relationships, marriage is a mirror. It's a reflection of how you see yourself." She pointed at both of them. "So, depending on the amount of love or hate you have for yourself; that is what you will experience in return from your spouse."

"So what happens in a marriage when one person sees themselves as a Christian and the other doesn't?" Kevin asked. "What does that reflect?"

"Good question son. Let's look into your mirror and find out." As Kevin tried to figure out what that could mean, Asè directed her attention to Tina. "So, Mrs. Smalls," she said,

"Tell me … what is the #1 thing you dislike about your husband?"

Tina scrunched her eyes. "I don't see what that has to do with—"

"Please honey." Asè held up her hand. "Just answer the question for me, okay?"

Tina blew her breath. "Ok. Well, if I had to pick just one thing it would be the way he talks to me. He is always prancing around his knowledge about different things and insulting me for not knowing as much as he does. He acts like I'm dumb."

"Does he speak to you about the bible?"

"He used to," Tina said. "For years he's been beating me in the head with the bible, telling me 'no' this verse means this and 'no' that verse means that. But now that he no longer believes in the bible like that, he beats me over the head with some type of African texts. And I don't be trying to hear it. So he ridicules me for not grasping it." Kneeling back in the chair looking at Kevin, she added, "It's like he gets a thrill from tearing me down."

Asè glanced at Kevin, noticing the pride written all over his face. It wasn't hard to tell that Tina's comments went right over his head. "I see," she said. "Well, has he always spoken to in this way?"

"Oh no. When I first met Kevin, he treated me like a queen. He spoke life into me. He inspired me to believe that I could escape the projects and become anything I wanted. He used to take me out to different museums and art galleries, exposing me to different cultures. "Once," she reminisced, "Kevin even threw me a surprise party when I graduated college and gave a speech in front of everybody about how smart and beautiful I was."

Kevin smiled, remembering the event.

"Aww," Asè replied. "That sounds night and day from the man you were describing to me earlier."

Tina nodded, holding back tears. "Yeah, it is. Back then he used to love me. Now all he cares about is them damn books," she said looking at Kevin. "Do you know we haven't slept in the same bed together in months? He falls asleep every night on the couch with a book in his hand ... and this was before he backslid."

Kevin shook his head. "Oh my God. This is some bullshit. Can I tell my side of the story now?"

The restaurant had become quite crowded since they first walked in. And the tone of Kevin's voice was so loud that it drew the attention of almost everyone around them, some of whom they had known. "Sure son," Asè answered. "But let's finish this outside."

Kevin and Tina walked towards the door so fast they forgot to pay the tab. So Asè left a fifty dollar bill on the table, then waved at Ella working the register. Ella smiled and nodded, and the trio was out the door.

The old woman led the Smalls towards a narrow sidewalk at the end of the plaza that overlooked the city's river. "Where are we going Asè?" Kevin asked from behind.

Ignoring his question, she walked up to a rail and leaned

up against it. Kevin and Tina made their way next to her and stood on each side. "Ok. The ball is now in your court Kevin." Asè peered into his eyes. "So tell me, pastor … What is the #1 thing you dislike about your wife?"

"Oh, that's easy. Her nagging," Kevin said without hesitation. "Every time I turn around, she nagging me about being a sinner. When I drink a beer, it's a sin. When I watch a non-Christian movie, it's a sin. When I read books of African spirituality, it's a sin. And anytime something goes wrong in the house with kids or finances or something, she blames me for it … talking about evil spirits are attached to me because I left Christ."

"Well, that sounds familiar," the old woman said, grinning.

"Ha-ha," Kevin said.

"But moving along," the old woman continued. "So how did Tina speak to you before you left your religion?"

"Well, she was a lot less nagging, but she still stayed on my case. For instance," he said, "Tina hates it when I go out to shoot hoops or play golf with my old buddies because she feels like I shouldn't have any non-Christian friends … she said it made me look bad as a pastor. So a lot of times I would just stay home so that I wouldn't have to hear her mouth."

"Is that true Tina?" Asè asked.

"Yes. The bible says not to be unequally yoked with unbelievers. And he knows that better than anybody because he used to preach it."

"Keyword—*used* to," Kevin replied.

"Yeah, it's a lotta things you used to be that you ain't no mo," Tina said.

"Well, at least I've changed. You've been the same since day one—a nagger."

Tina reached out her arm trying to slap Kevin in the face, but Asè stood in the way. "Calm down sweetie."

"Forget this." Tina threw up her hands and she began walking away.

Immediately, Asè turned to Kevin and gave him the side-eye. "Well if she is such a nagger Mr. smalls, then why did you marry her?"

"Because I love her," he said. Tina stopped and slowly turned around.

"You do?" Asè asked. "Well, you sure have a way of showing it. I haven't heard you say one nice thing about your wife all day."

"Humph," Kevin uttered. "Now you sound like her."

Asè patted him on the back. "Well answer me this Kevin. What was it that made you fall in love with Tina?"

"Because she believed in me," Kevin said, staring into Tina's eyes. Then he looked to his left at the old woman. "See, I was a young knucklehead running the streets before I met Tina. She told me I was the smartest man she knew and encouraged me to change my life," he smiled. "Had I not met her, I probably would've been a statistic."

Tina smiled as tears fell down her cheeks.

Asè grabbed Kevin's hand and walked him over to his

wife. Then she stepped back to face them both. "I have one last question. But this one is for both of you." Without waiting for their response, she continued. "You two have a lot of issues that have been swept under the rug for many years. But if you had the chance to be granted one wish that would save your marriage and make your ladder days together better than the past, would you take it?"

Both Tina and Kevin looked at each other waiting for the other to speak up first, and then finally each nodded and said, "Yes."

Asè clapped her hands once, but loudly. "Great! Because I'm going to grant you that wish today. And it won't take long because all you two really lack is discernment."

Tina sucked her teeth and opened her mouth to speak but Asè interrupted her. "No mam," she said. "You already had your chance to talk. Now it's my turn. So be quiet and listen honey." Tina was beside herself, but she remained silent.

"From both of your perspectives, you see each other as the problem," Asè said. "But like I told you earlier, a marriage is a mirror of your relationship with yourself. So the problem you see in your spouse is a reflection of the problem *you fail* to see in yourself. Follow me on this."

"You"—Asè pointed to Tina—"don't feel loved by your God. You're always trying to keep his commandments to please him, but always messing up. So you constantly feel condemned by him. And because of this, you treat Kevin the same way. You call him a sinner and condemn him to the same hell that you fear you might end up at."

Kevin looked at Tina wondering if what Asè said was true. Tina turned away, feeling both embarrassed and relieved at the same time.

"And you mister," Asè said pointing at Kevin. "You don't feel like you're smart enough in comparison to your wife and other folks who graduated from college. So you're always reading books and trying to share how much you know with others to prove to them that you are smart. This is why you treat Tina as if she's slow because that's how you feel about yourself."

Tina's jaw dropped. She had no idea that *Mr. Know-it-all* felt as dumb as her. Kevin folded his arms and his face became red.

"I'm not trying to embarrass you son. I'm just trying to straighten out your vision." The old woman reached in her bag and pulled out a small hand-held mirror with gold frames. "Look in the mirror," she said, holding it up facing Kevin. "Now, look at yourself and name one flaw that you notice?"

Kevin seemed disinterested, but he went along. "Uh, I guess this—"

"No guessing son," Asè interrupted. "Just tell me what blemishes you see on yourself."

"Ok. I see this ketchup stain on my shirt." He pulled a napkin from his pocket and began wiping.

"Exactly. And now you will see my point." Asè proclaimed. "When you notice something you don't like in the mirror; you don't try to change the mirror. You simply fix the problem that the mirror shows you to have. Why? Because you recognize that the mirror is only a reflection of your flaws, not the flaw itself. And the same goes for your marriage. You two are a reflection of your flaws, but not the flaw itself."

Kevin's head flipped back in awe. "WOW!" he said. "I have to admit … that's pretty impressive Asè … I never saw it like that before."

She placed her hand on his shoulder. "False information clouds one's vision. But the truth sets the eyes free." She smiled and winked.

"Hold on." Tina blurted out. "I feel what you saying about all this reflection stuff Asè, but Kevin still left the faith … Now I can admit to having some issues with how God feels about me, but at least I still believe in Him. But Kevin—he doesn't. So, how can we reconcile our marriage if only one of us believes in God?" She twitched her head from right to left.

"Well, has Kevin told you that he doesn't believe in God?"

"Uh … No," Tina said, surprised by her answer.

"So why do you think that he doesn't?"

"Because he doesn't believe in Jesus Christ anymore, Tina answered. "And can't nobody get to God except through him."

The old woman grinned. "Well, I don't mean to burst your bubble Tina, but Jesus is only a concept—not a person. He was invented by the Romans based on the story of Horus from ancient Egypt."

"See. That's what I've been trying to tell you, Tina."

Kevin shouted.

She shook her head in disbelief. "I don't know about all this. I mean if Jesus ain't real, then how come I'm able to cast out demons in his name? Tell me that?" Tina demanded.

"Whatever you believe to be true is what you will experience," Asè answered. "To a child who believes in Santa Claus, that's who brought them their gifts. But in reality, it was their parents."

Tina thought about that statement carefully before responding. "But what about God? Are you insinuating that there is no God?"

"Oh, no honey. I wouldn't dare make that claim. We all know a higher power is responsible for this beautiful creation. But that power doesn't live in the sky—it lives in you. So, you are God. And so is Kevin … and every other living being on the planet. But in order to see God in others, you have to first see God in yourself."

Tina and Kevin both looked into each other's eyes with hope. Seeing the understanding finally beginning to show on Tina's face, Asè felt encouraged to continue. "Believe it or not, this is why you two are together; to help each other see God. But since God is love, y'all have to learn how to love yourselves first so that you can reflect it towards each other."

Asè paused briefly to let that sink in, before continuing with her lesson. "Young lady," she said to Tina. "Your husband truly loves you and wants to stay married to you forever. He just wants you to believe in him the way you believe in Christ. The beating you over the head with knowledge is just his way of trying to regain your faith in him."

"And you son," she said to Kevin. "Your wife loves you to death. She doesn't want to divorce you. She just wants you to go back to being her partner instead of her lecturer. The divorce papers were just the only way she knew how to get your attention. You just couldn't see that because of your need to be right all of the time."

The Smalls stood there vulnerable with their hearts shown on their face. Tears slowly dripped from Tina's eyes. "You know, she's right." She looked up at Kevin. "I never wanted a divorce. I just didn't know what else to do."

"I don't want one either baby," Kevin confessed. "Never did and never will." Tina walked towards Kevin and embraced him with a hug.

"I'm so sorry," Tina whispered in his ear.

"Me too, Tee-tee," Kevin replied. "I can't believe we were about to end it all over this."

"I can." Asè laughed. "Now you see how important it is to have discernment?"

"I sure do," Tina replied. "Thanks, Asè."

Tina and Kevin tried to continue the conversation with Asè, but she insisted that her time was up. After constantly refusing their offers of transportation—she excused herself and began walking west. The Smalls watched her go, realizing that they knew nothing about the old woman or if they would ever see her again.

"I guess all the rumors about her were true after all," Tina uttered as Asè disappeared from their sight.

"What rumors?" Kevin asked.

"The ones about her being divine."

FOUR

I WALKED INSIDE THE BOOKSTORE AS BABA WAS ringing up a customer. When he peeped it was me, he lit up with joy. "DC!" he said, stepping back. "Is that you boy?"

"Damn. You done forgot what I look like already?" I said walking forward.

Baba put his glasses on and looked at me closer. "Oh no, I remember that big ass head of yours anywhere. Just wasn't expecting to get a visit from Mr. Hollywood, that's all."

I laughed, as he came from around the counter to dab me up with a hug. "Hey Baba."

He looked me up and down like a proud dad. "Man, it's good to see you boy. So how long you been back?"

"About a week or so."

Baba's face quickly tightened up. "And you just now coming to see me?" he asked.

"C'mon man. You know I gotta make my rounds."

"Humph," he mumbled. "So I guess I'm at the end of

your "to see" list, huh?" he said sarcastically.

"Ah. Here we go," I replied.

When I was younger, Baba always lectured me on the importance of keeping in contact with one's elders. He would quote of Asè's sayings, to 'never put those who came before you at the end of your priorities.' And for that, I was indeed guilty.

Then the phone rings, breaking his attention. He puts his fist up at me, playfully, before heading back around the counter. "Hold on. I'll deal with you in a minute."

"Peace, love, and black power. This is Baba's. How may I help you?"

I couldn't hear what the other person on the phone was saying, but whatever it was, had saddened Baba. He fell to his chair, like a balloon that just got popped. "Are you sure it can't be reversed? Maybe you need to get a second opinion?" Baba asked the caller. Moments later, a tear fell down his cheek, so I assumed the answer was no.

After Baba hung up the phone, he told me that his younger brother was diagnosed with cancer and seemed very mentally unstable. I chatted with him for a few, trying to keep his spirits up, but he was distracted by the customers walking in and out of the store. Eventually, I told him I was there to meet Asè and excused myself over to the café.

THE SOUNDS OF ERYKAH BADU WAS BUMPING

from the speakers as Asè strolled inside the Café, where I had been waiting. I was sitting on the sofa by the wall, reading a new book I had purchased, when she approached.

She gave me a warm embrace and then sat down to my left. We talked for hours, mostly about my life since she had been gone. Mid-way through the convo, I realized I was talking too much so I tried to redirect the subject back to where she had been at all these years. But all she would give me was "I've been around." And when I asked her why she left me, she responded with a parable. "A seed has to be left in the dirt and covered in darkness to grow and reach the light."

Responses like that pissed me off—like can you just answer my damn question—but I was so happy to see her again that I just let it ride.

I bragged to Asè about all the money I had made from my writing and the two houses I owned, one in LA and the other here in Columbia. And though she congratulated me on my success, I felt bad about not telling her the full truth. The truth about me being a one-hit-wonder in the film industry and my LA home in the process of being foreclosed. But I didn't want to seem like a failure to the woman who inspired my success, so I kept it to myself.

"So how do you know the Smalls?" I asked.

Leaning forward, the old woman said in a playful tone, "The same way I know you, son." After a brief pause, she added, "They were lacking discernment."

I smiled, knowing where this convo was headed.

As Asè proceeded to tell me about the issues between

Tina and Kevin, she interrupted herself to explain that she wasn't breaking confidence; she was teaching a lesson. "And besides … they'll be sharing with everyone around here what they learned anyways."

After she laid out the concept of marriage being a mirror of how individuals felt about themselves, I asked her if this same rule applied to all relationships. "Yep. They sure do." Asè answered. "Everyone sees in others, what they see in themselves; because we are one." She then pointed towards my eyes. "But what they see depends on which mirror they're looking into."

"Huh?" I prompted. "Whatchu mean by *which* mirror—I thought it was only one?"

"Oh no, son" she said. "According to our ancient ancestors, there are seven types of mirrors that we see life through. The mirror that Tina and Kevin were looking through is just the first one."

"Oh ok," I said. "So what are the other mirrors?"

Well, the second mirror," Asè began, "is the one that reflects what we judge. This is usually something we have an emotional charge with; something we have either been wounded by in the past; or something we simply hate because it goes against nature. But what most people are unaware of is that, regardless of *why* we may judge something, if we place enough energy towards it, we will attract that very same thing into our lives."

"Oh. So it's just like that saying 'you are what you attract' right?"

She shook her head gently. "No, son. That's a European concept." Asè pointed to the wall in front of us, featuring a mural of ancient Egyptian art. "Remember," she said. "In African culture, we are magnetic beings comprised of spiritual energy. So, we don't attract to us what we are, we attract the frequency we are vibrating on." As I nodded with interest, she further explained.

"This means the stronger your emotions are towards something, the likelier you will draw it to you. So, if you have a strong hate for a person, a mentality, or a lifestyle," she said, "you will attract those very same energies into your life in some form or fashion."

I rubbed my chin, stroking my beard, soaking in the knowledge. "So if I don't like something, then how do I avoid attracting it to me?"

"Simple," she proclaimed. "By not judging it."

"But how do you not judge something that you don't like?" I asked.

"Well," she said, "You have to heal the wound within that causes you to place judgment on things without."

I leaned in closer for an explanation.

"Ya see, Dane," she continued. "You are a great writer and producer. No one can argue that. But your judgment against those who think differently from you is stunting your career."

"What?" I said defensibly, wondering if she knew my situation. "My movies are still making money, so I don't know what you talking bout."

Asè smiled at my pride. "True indeed," she said. "But when was your last blockbuster?"

"About five years ago," I sighed, "when *It Takes A Village* came out."

Nodding and placing her hand over mines, she asked, "And why do you think that is?"

I shrugged. "I don't know. Some movies are hits and others are not. That's just how it goes."

"Hmm." She pondered. "Well, that's not the case for Singleton. All his movies are hits."

"Yeah, but that's different," I said. "He got Hollywood backing him. I'm independent."

"What about Harris?" she asked. "He's independent and all of his movies are successful. Some are even on Netflix."

"Hold up. You watch Netflix, Asè?"

"Yeah chile, I like movies too." She grinned. "And I've seen many hit movies on there by black filmmakers. So, why do you think they didn't purchase your last few releases?"

"Because I'm a revolutionary," I answered. "I write about the type of shit that challenges white supremacy and the industry doesn't support that ..."

I disagree," Asè interjected. "There are many black movies out there just as revolutionary as yours. You just can't see it, because you lack discernment."

"C'mon Asè," I shouted. "Really?"

"Yes son," she said, frowning at my attitude. "Not every movie has to be about black power for it to challenge white supremacy. In this society where we're constantly being negatively portrayed in the media, any movie that shows black people in a positive light breaks that narrative. And there are a growing number of filmmakers, who are doing just that."

I sighed with disappointment that Asè was not on my side.

Looking at my blank expression, she smiled at me with compassion. "Let me ask you something, son. Have any of your contemporaries ever told you something like 'your script is too narrow' or 'it's not universal enough'?"

"Yeah, all the time," I said. "My script reviewers and Network execs have been saying this to me for years ... trying to get me to alter my scripts and make them more *appealing*." I held my two fingers up on my left and right hand, for quotations. "But I'm like I'm not trying to reach the masses; I'm just trying to reach my people."

"Once again your perception is off, son. It's not that they want you to appeal to other races—they just want you to at least appeal to more people within your own race."

I raised my eyebrows. "Whatchu mean?"

"The audience you write for is too limited," she answered. "You write for people who are into Pan-Africanism, black history, and indigenous spirituality like you. And that's great. But the majority of Africans in America are not into that. So by you constantly creating characters in your stories who represent the smallest portion of the black community, you're unable to appeal to the rest."

I put my hand on my head. "Dang, that makes hella

sense," I said. "But what am I supposed to do? Dumb my content down so the rest can get it?"

"No, son. You just need to expand your worldview."

"Enlighten me then," I said. "What am I not seeing?"

She smiled, happy to teach me a new lesson. "Well, like all humans," she said, "black people consist of many different personalities and go through many different experiences. So you have to include these personalities and experiences in your characters so the rest of the community can relate to them. You did that with your first movie, remember? That's why it was such a big hit because it appealed to so many different people."

"Yeah," I said slowly. "Even white folks loved the film ... which surprised the hell outta me."

"Well, the human experience is universal," she replied. "So anyone can enjoy a black story, just as you can enjoy a white story." She then folded her leg across her lap and looked over at me sternly as if she was about to give me the message of a lifetime. And she did.

"Your problem is you don't accept people for who they are," she divulged. "You want everybody to think just like you. And this shows up in your stories. Instead of just allowing the characters you create to be the people they are based on—you interject your personality onto them so they can carry your thoughts. And this makes your movies dull and un-relatable."

My mouth stood wide open for a few seconds. I felt like I had been hit with a ton of bricks. "Man," I dropped back in the chair, "I can't believe I wasn't able to see all of this."

She reached over the table stand in between our chairs and gently placed her hand over mines. "It's alright, son. We all lose sight of truth from time to time."

"True," I said. "And at least now I know why my last few films flopped." Then, leaning back meditating on what I just said, I had a revelation. "Well, how bout that?" I muttered. "Here I was blaming the industry … when I should have been blaming the man in the mirror."

"The law of mirrors ain't about blaming anyone, son. It's just there to show you what wounds you need to heal."

"Oh yeah. I remember you said something about that earlier." Leaning my head over to towards Asè, I asked, "Any idea what my wounds are?"

"Well, usually when one rejects others for thinking differently than them, it signifies that they've been treated the same way in the past, by those who thought differently from them. So, you tell me son?" she said. "Have you felt rejected by anyone close to you in the past?"

As I folded my arms, almost immediately, my mom came across my mind and how even to this day she rejects me for not adhering to her religion of Christianity. My face began to harden and my eyes became watery. Then I quickly regathered myself and responded, "Yeah. My mother," I confessed.

Asè hopped out of her chair like a spring, reached down, and embraced me with a motherly hug. "That's it right there son. That's the wound you need to heal. So forgive her and let it go because it's killing both you and your career."

Looking up at the old woman, I asked, "But how can I

forgive her … I mean what kinda mom rejects her children?"

"The type of mom that was rejected by her mother," she answered. "You may not realize it son, but your mom is human just like you. And she endured the same pain that you're experiencing now … which could be why she is so fervid about her beliefs."

Hearing Asè break things down for me put things in perspective. As she continued to ramble on, I daydreamed briefly, considering that maybe my mom was just as broken as me. When I came back to reality, I heard Asè talking, saying, "So it's not because she doesn't love you. It's just that … she's just too indoctrinated to see what you see."

"So in other words," I said, "she just lacks discernment?"

"Bingo." She winked out of her right eye.

For the next half-hour, I picked Asè's brain about the other 5 mirrors of reflection. Then halfway through our convo, my wife had called to remind me that I was supposed to pick up my son from summer camp today. I wanted to stay with Asè a little longer, but it was already thirty minutes to four, so I had to leave now to make it to camp in time.

"Asè, you sure you don't want to ride with me?" I asked. "You can meet my son and I can drop you off anywhere you like me too after that."

"I would love to son, I really would," she replied. "But I have another session here in a few. Business is booming around these parts." We both laughed out loud. Then she grabbed her famous duffle bag and walked me outside.

As I was opening the car door to my Range Rover, I

looked up at her and asked, "So when I'm a see you again Asè?"

"I don't know when son," she answered. "But I'll be around for a while. So keep a lookout for me." Then she pointed at the iPhone watch on my wrist. "Now go and get your son so that he doesn't feel rejected!"

FIVE

ASÈ HAD JUST GOT OFF THE CITY BUS ON LAKE Murray Blvd. and began walking towards the dam overlooking the lake. This was the second bus she had taken since leaving Liberty Heights, about thirty-five minutes west. As she reached the walkway's entry point, she stopped to admire the view of the lake and watched the sunset. Then she grabbed her bag and continued walking.

After reaching the end of the walkway by the parking lot, Asè glanced around as if she was looking for something, then heard a chirp from a swallow bird posted comfortably on top of the gate. She greeted the bird with a smile, and it responded with a sweet gurgle sound before flying away. Asè walked over to a bench nearby, placed her bag in her lap, and rested her head against the gate behind it. As she dozed off, the evening sky turned black, and the passerby chatting faded away.

Although it was a safe area, people rarely walked this path

after dark . . .

DR. TOMMY HEMMITT HAD NEVER BEEN TO THE dam in his life, even though he lived five minutes away from it. And he wouldn't have come tonight if it wasn't for the burning thoughts of despair that plagued his mind. As he pulled into the parking lot in his khaki-colored Mercedes Benz, he began to think about his life.

Tommy was a middle-aged pharmacist and a widower going on four years now. He had moved from Liberty Heights to Irmo after his wife's death in hopes of a fresh start. Only whites and rich blacks lived out here, so he figured it would be much safer living among the haves rather than the have-nots for a change. After all, nothing was more important than safety; and only money could buy that. That had been Tommy's motto ever since his wife died—until earlier that day when he received some news that shattered his security.

He had been experiencing burning sensations, so he went to get checked out. His doctor informed him that he was in the early stages of prostate cancer, but if they started chemo right away, they could save him. But Tommy remembered the horrific death it caused his wife, and hopelessly declined. And he had been depressed ever since.

But tonight, the pharmacist had reached an all-time low. He was contemplating suicide.

As Tommy walked up the short hill onto the dam's dark

walkway, he tripped over someone's foot, extending about a yard off the path. "What the hell?" Tommy shouted as he fell to the ground. "You need to watch where you're going, lady?" He said as he got up.

"I'm sorry young man, I didn't mean to hurt ya," the old woman said. "But you're the only one moving, son. So maybe you need to watch where you're going."

Man, this lady must be high. I thought all the bums lived in Liberty Heights. Shaking his head, he replied, "Whatever you say, ma'am. Then he brushed off his clothes and continued walking. And fast.

About twenty yards or so into his walk, he stopped to look back at the old woman. She smiled at him and held up her hand with a short wave. He thought about his wife and how she would feel if a man had spoken to her that way. But he hated talking to strangers, so when he found himself turning around heading her way, he mumbled, "What the hell am I doing?"

When he reached the bench where the old woman was sitting, she got up to greet him. "Hey there, son. You alright?"

Tommy quickly noticed the gold on her fingers, then the matching pieces around her neck. *Hmm. This lady ain't no bum. She looks like royalty.* He peered into her eyes and replied, "Yeah. I'm ok. How are you?" Before the old woman could respond, he added, "I apologize for my behavior. It's just been a rough day, that's all."

"Oh, I'm fine, son. That was water under the bridge as soon as it happened."

Asè pointed at the water flowing under the bridge and laughed. Tommy thought it was funny, too but held in his laughter in.

Asè then grabbed her bag from the bench and began walking down the down. "C'mon," she said.

Tommy stood still for a few seconds before he began walking. After catching up with her, he asked, "So, what are you doing out here this late, ma'am?"

"Oh, I just came out here to witness a better perception," she answered.

Tommy assumed she was talking about the view. As they crossed the first light pole, Asè looked up at Tommy as if she saw him for the first time. "Hey … You're Dr. Hemmitt, ain't it? I thought that was you."

"Uh … do I know you?" Tommy said, scrunching up his face.

"Nope, but I know you," she said. "I've seen you many times in Liberty Heights. And I know quite a few people who go to your pharmacy."

"Oh, ok. So you live in Liberty Heights?" Tommy asked.

The old woman nodded and reached her hand out. "I AM Asè. No Mrs. to it. Just Asè."

Tommy shook her hand but was still a little leery. "Well, you a long way from home, ain't you?" he asked."

"I could say the same about you, son. What are you doing way out here at this time of night?"

"Oh. I don't live in Liberty Heights. I stay down the street from here," he said with pride. Then he realized he had just told a complete stranger where he lived and frowned.

"Pretty nice area. You must like it out here?" Asè asked.

Looking away from the old woman, he replied, "It's ok." She noticed that Tommy was short for words, so she tried another tactic.

"This view sort of reminds me of Charleston," Asè had blurted. "I remember one night, I was walking downtown near the bridge, and I saw a young woman leave her kids in the car chasing after a twenty dollar bill in the street," she said. "As she reached for the money, a young man had hopped in her car and drove off with her kids. She jumped in the left lane to chase after him, but got hit by a car and died instantly."

Tommy turned his head enraged. "What the hell? Why would you tell me a story like that?"

She shrugged her shoulders innocently. "I didn't mean to offend you. I just always found it interesting, ya know?"

"What?" Tommy asked.

Facing him, she replied, "How people risk their lives chasing after dead presidents for safety."

The two strolled down the walkway in silence for a couple of minutes. Tommy looked to his left, squinting his eyes at the blinding headlights of the cars dashing across the bridge. He did all he could to keep his eyes off the old woman who had just pulled his card, but the burden of guilt became too suppressed. After a heavy sigh, Tommy took his hands out of his pocket and replied, "Yep, that's me. Always chasing money."

Asè patted him on the back of his shoulder. "That's many

people, son. Not just you. But since you confessed," she said with a smile, "Why are you chasing after it with all the money you have?"

Tommy looked at her and then turned away quickly. *Why am I talking to a stranger?* The only strangers he would ever converse with were the ones that came in his office. Other than that, he kept it moving. Yet, here Tommy was, about to reveal his innermost thoughts to a woman wearing a dress that was not even made in America. He couldn't put his finger on it, but her presence made him feel safe. So he relaxed and sung like a bird.

Tommy told Asè about growing up in foster care with his older brother Baba after being abandoned by their parents. Then he talked about his wife, and all he did to keep her alive, and the son they had in Atlanta, which he ran off due to his overprotective ways. And on and on he went, sharing his heart with a stranger in the dark.

TOMMY WAS ON HIS THIRD CUP OF COFFEE AT the IHOP across the street by the time he had told Asè his life story. He was drinking a double shot expresso, while Asè sipped on sipped a hot chocolate, made with almond milk at her request. Free from the worries and fears of cancer, Tommy was having the time of his life. He felt like he was talking to the mother he never had.

"So," Tommy said, "I kinda felt like a failure when Linda

got cancer. I mean, I'm a doctor, for Christ's sake." He shook his head.

"Yeah, it sure would have been nice if she had a healer around to save her." The old woman laughed out oud innocently. But Tommy didn't find it funny. As he was about to explode, Asè raised both of her hands straight up, signaling for Tommy to relax. "*Calmmmm* down, I'm just messing with you, chile. I know you did all you could."

Tommy was unsure if he was being insulted or not.

"But on a serious note," Asè continued, "Your wife has been dead for more than four years, Tommy. And here you are, still allowing yourself to suffer from the decisions that she made. You shouldn't blame yourself for other people's mistakes."

Tommy looked confused. "What do you mean by mistakes?" Tommy raised his voice. "It wasn't her fault she got cancer."

"Oh really? Then who's fault, was it?" she asked gently.

Tommy leaned forward, with scolding eyes. "Hold on. So you blaming my wife for contracting cancer?"

"No, son. I don't believe in the blame game. I'm just asking you a question. Who caused your wife to get cancer?"

"No one did; she had breast cancer. It's the most common cancer among black women." He shrugged his shoulders as if to say *everyone knows this*. "Some women get it, and others don't. But my wife did. Case closed."

"You make cancer sound like it's a cold, son." The old lady smiled lightly. "Like it's something that you catch, rather than something you attract."

Tommy didn't understand her point, nor was he trying to. "Well, I've been a health practitioner for over twenty years, so I believe I know a thing or two about how people get cancer."

"Fair enough," Asè said. "I know nothing about western medicine, so you got me right there." Then she folded her right leg over the other, still underneath the table, and leaned back the chair. "But what I am familiar with is Mother Nature. You know anything about that, Dr. Hemmitt?"

He folded his lips. "Mother Nature? You mean the trees, plants, and animals?"

"Yep, but more so about how she functions. You know ... like the healing properties that exist within the plants and all that good stuff?"

"No, not really," he answered. "I mean, I heard about 'em, but that's not something we're really taught in medical school. That's what naturopathic doctor's study."

"You don't have to go to school to figure out nature doc. All you have to do is study yourself."

"What do you mean?" Tommy asked.

"Well, nature is us! It's where we all come from; so it's what we all are. No different than a child being the fruit of their parents. Though they are individuals, they are still one. And so are we with nature. Therefore, the study of nature is the study of self."

Feeling too overqualified to be having this conversation, Tommy just nodded and smiled. "Ohhh ... kay."

"So being that we are one with nature," Asè continued,

"Our bodies require that we feed it what grows in nature to function at our best. When we don't do that and eat things that are man-made, we end up with diseases like cancer." After a quick pause, she raised her index finger in the air. "But just like nature is designed to heal itself, so are we."

"Oh. I see where you're going," Tommy said. "You one of those new-age teachers who believe that nature heals all, huh?"

"No, what I teach is ancient, son. It's the same universal law that our ancestors used to live by before we adopted the ways of Europeans."

"Now you sound like Baba," Tommy said, shaking his head. "But this is 2020, so what worked back then doesn't necessarily work today. We are evolved beings. So, the medicines had to evolve as well. We no longer have to go out into the bush and study plants all day," he teased. "We now have the man-power and technology to offer treatments to people; that is far more advanced than the 'root doctors' from back in the day."

Asè smiled, took a sip of her hot chocolate, and folded her hands on top of the table. "You young folks' trip me out, doc. Y'all are so in love with modern conveniences that you are unable to see the damage that it's doing to society, especially us."

Tommy's face looked like he was sucking a lemon. "The damages?" he shouted. "No disrespect Asè, but that's not true. As I said, I've been in the field for over twenty years. And I have treated more people over the last ten years than I have my first ten years. And this is the result of those," he moved his fingers in quotations, "modern conveniences," as you say."

"Oh really?" she asked. "Well, what do you mean by the word "treat" doc?

"You know … to heal and to cure," he replied.

"Well, if that's the case doc, then why weren't you or your counterparts able to treat your wife?" she asked softly.

Tommy's face turned dim. Feeling even guiltier than before, he turned his head toward the window, and his eyes became watery. Asè reached her hand across the table, touching his. "Your wife's death was not your fault, son. And I'm not here to point the finger. I'm here to show you a different way."

Slowly turning his head back to the direction of Asè, he asked, "What kinda way?"

"A way that leads to life," she whispered as if she was keeping a secret. "A way that is much more fruitful than the path your wife took."

Tommy's eyebrow raised in confusion. "And how are you going to do that?" He asked in disbelief.

"I'm a Perceptionist," she proclaimed. Before she could get the next sentence out, Tommy interrupted.

"A what?" he asked.

"A Perceptionist," she said. "I perceive things about life that most people miss. It is my gift. And this gift has brought me to you. I am here to tell you how to save your life. You do, want to remain alive at least another decade, don't you?"

Tommy still had no idea where the old lady was going

with her spiel, but he was curious. "Of course," he said.

"Great! Let's do it then." Asè rubbed her hands together with excitement. "But first, let me ask you a question." Tommy leaned forward in anticipation, motioning for her to proceed. "Now, don't take this the wrong way, son. This is only a question, ok?" He nodded suspiciously.

"Why was it that you disagreed with taking chemotherapy?"

"Wait a minute. How did you know this?" Tommy asked. "I didn't tell you that."

"I told you doc. I'm a Perceptionist."

"No for real Asè. How did you know that?"

"I already told you, son. Now, are you going to answer my question or not?" she asked kindly.

"Aw, what the hell," Tommy said. "Well, chemo had drained my wife's life. It zapped her of her energy, took away her hair, and made her skin darker—and not in a good way. It brought her to the point where she was less than a hundred pounds." He stopped for a moment to wipe his eyes. "After seeing what that process had done to her, I didn't want anything to do with it."

"Ah, I see," Asè replied. "Well, I don't blame ya. No one should have to endure such trauma." As Tommy nodded, fighting back tears, Asè reached for his hand. "But tell me this doc. How was your wife's health before she began chemo?"

Tommy lifted his head and began reminiscing. "Oh, she was in much better shape. She had all her hair, worked out every morning, and was still full of life." He smiled.

"Hmm. Well, if you don't mind me asking doc, why was it that you guys decided for her to undergo chemo?"

"Because our doctor said that it was the best thing to do. He told us that we had caught her cancer just in time. And that if we started chemo right away ..." Tommy paused, looking as if he was trying to solve a mystery, then finished his sentence, "We could save her life." He then glanced out the window, shaking his head. "Wow."

Asè perceived his thoughts. "Is that what he told you too?"

"Yep, word for word," Tommy answered.

"Well, that's the typical approach for western doctors. For some strange reason, they believe that unnatural means is the best way to cure a natural body." She shrugged her shoulders. "And because you're a chemist, you believed his diagnosis, right?"

"Uh ... yeah. I mean ... I've seen many of my customers go through chemo and beat cancer. So I figured it would be the same with my wife, ya know?" He shook his head. "But, it wasn't."

"Well, chemotherapy is not a hit or miss approach, doc. I know it seems to work well for some and not so well for others, but in reality, it doesn't work well for anyone." The old woman took another sip from her cup, then said, "You see. The body is not designed to consume chemicals or radiation—especially not the high doses that are given to patients during chemotherapy—because they kill off the blood cells that the body needs to survive."

"No, they don't," Tommy interrupted. "They kill off the cancer cells and tumors that are causing cancer. That's the whole point of chemo treatments. How else they would beat cancer?" he asked condescendingly.

"Son. The body naturally kills off cancer cells on its own. It doesn't need chemo to do that." Seeing the arrogance and disbelief polished all over his face, Asè changed her approach. "Have you ever read Dr. Sheng's research?" she asked.

Tommy jerked his head up like he had seen a ghost. "How you know Dr. Sheng?"

"I never said I knew him. I said, have you read his research?"

"Not since college," he answered. "He was my professor."

"Well, you should," she said. "His latest research was published in the New York Times, proving to you what I just said. He also stated that almost the entire American population has cancer cells existing within them, but only 50% of the population gets cancer."

Tommy raised his eyebrows. "Huh? I don't get it. How could some get it and some don't; if we all have the cancer cells in us?"

"Well, according to your professor, it's because only half of the country has a properly functioning immune system. You see, when you eat natural foods, you give the body the nutrients that it needs to build a healthy immune system. But you know that from studying biology, right?"

"Yeah," he said. "The immune system is what fights off

diseases," he said with his shoulders raised and chest out.

"Exactly. So if your immune system is shot, then you wouldn't be able to fight off the cells that cause cancer, right?"

Tommy was floored. After all his years of practice, He couldn't believe he never grasped this simple concept before. He then leaned forward, with his hand stroking his beard, and said to himself out loud, "Damn. So we really don't need chemotherapy."

She shook her head. "Nope. It's unnatural and does more harm than good."

"How so," he asked.

"Well, for one, it kills off both the cancer cells and the healthy cells. So the body is depleted of what it needs to survive—the cells—and goes into fight or flight mode to stay alive. This is why everyone in chemotherapy looks like they're in the middle of a war because they are. And the ones who survive it, do so because of their lifestyle changes—not by the chemo itself."

"What you mean … their diet?" Tommy asked.

"Yeah, mostly," she answered. "Like I told you earlier, the body is designed to heal itself. We just have to feed it what it's designed to eat. You know … water, plants, fruits, nuts, seeds, and all that good stuff found in nature. Why do you think this makes up what most cancer patients eat while they are going through chemo?"

The pharmacist was finally comprehending the old lady. Although it was contrary to his training, it made good sense, he reasoned. "So basically, you suggesting that we should all be vegans, right?"

"Oh no, I'm not against people eating animals. All life consumes life to survive," she said while placing her hands over her chest. "But if you want to heal your body, then only nature can *help* you do that, doc." She smiled innocently.

Tommy thought about his wife. He remembered the doctors recommending vegan options during her last stages of chemo before she died. He wondered if she could have been saved if she had started a little earlier.

"Hey doc, are you still with us?" Asè said, waving her hand side to side.

Tommy laughed at himself for being caught daydreaming. "Yeah, he replied. "So Asè, if eating a nature-based diet can cure cancer, then it should also be able to prevent it then, right?"

"Bingo!" she said. "Now you using that African brain of yours. See how that one works better than the European one they gave you?" She grinned.

Tommy laughed out loud at the old woman. "I guess so," he said.

"Ain't no guessing about it, son. The most intelligent mind you have is the one connected to your bloodline. That other one you have causes confusion."

Tommy was spellbound by her statement. It was so simple, yet so profound, he thought. "So you think I could really reverse my cancer if I change my diet, Asè?"

"Chile please." She blew her hand and looked away. "I

don't think you will—I know you will," she proclaimed. "You know Mrs. Johnson, right?"

"Uhh … you talking about Ella who runs the 'Vegan Soul Bar'?"

Asè nodded.

"Yeah. We went to school together," Tommy. answered.

"Well, did you know she used to have breast cancer?"

Tommy's eyes spread wide as the ocean. "No. For real?"

"She sure did," Asè said. "Eating all 'em ribs, burgers, macaroni and cheese and all that other stuff y'all call soul food, caught up with her." She pointed at the menu on the wall. "But after she was diagnosed, she went to Spinx Raw on Two Notch, and they put her on a herbal detox program—and in 4 months, she was cancer-free."

"For real?" he asked.

"Yep. So after that, she stopped eating animals and cooking them for others."

"Ohhhhh," he said. "So, that's why Ella changed Soul Hub to the Vegan Soul Bar?" Asè nodded. "Man. I always wondered why she went from soul food to vegan food."

"Well, now you know," she replied. "And the same way Mother Nature healed her, she can heal you too."

Immediately, the vibration of hope and joy spread throughout Tommy's body; something he hadn't felt in years. But before he could open his mouth to express his gratitude, Asè raised her finger to continue. "But know this doc. Your diet is not only what you eat. It's what you watch, listen to, read, and do. So be mindful of what you are consuming on all levels."

"Will do," Tommy replied. He smiled, gazing at the old woman as if he was sitting across from an angel. Then he jumped up, walked over, and gave her a huge hug. "Thank you so much Asè," he said sincerely. "You know, had I not ran into you tonight, I probably would've—"

"Good to meet ya too, Tommy," Asè interrupted. "And good thing my foot wasn't the bridge, right?"

Staring into her eyes, Tommy wondered if she knew his plans beforehand. Then he nodded and excused himself to the bathroom.

A few minutes later, Tommy walked back to the booth and found both sides' empty, the tab paid for, and a book on the table. He picked it up and skimmed the cover, which read: *Ancient African Wisdom for Health of Mind, Body, and Spirit.* Then he looked up and saw Asè waving at him through the window as she hopped into an Uber.

SIX

I HAD BEEN DROPPING OFF FLYERS ALL DAY TO promote my annual film workshop, at different places in my old hood. "Do you know Asè?" Jamal Crews asked me as I was handing him more flyers to hang up. Jamal was the owner of Crews Community Center, the only place left where both youth and parents could participate in recreational activities since King Park had closed down.

"Yeah, I know her," I answered, peeping down the hall in the gift shop where Asè stood leaning against the counter surrounded by a bunch of teens. They were all laughing, both boys and girls, hanging on to the old woman's every word as if it were gold. "Who are all the kids with her?"

"That's our summer staff. I always hire the youth during the summers to keep them out these streets."

"That's what's up man. I wish I had something like this when I was their age."

"Yeah, they supposed to be getting the shop ready for

tonight's color painting class. But as you can see, Asè has them occupied." He grinned.

"Yeah I see," I said, smiling, thinking about how lucky those kids were to be in her presence at such a young age. "So, how do you know Asè?" I asked.

"My pops knew her," Jamal answered, still glancing down the hall at the loud flock of youth surrounding the old woman. "He told me before he and my mom had me, Asè helped saved their marriage." Jamal turned to me with a straight, emotionless face. "It didn't seem to be a big deal, though. She just helped him see the missing piece to the puzzle, he told me. "But pops never forgot about it. Or her."

"Man, that lady has the gift of gab, ain't it?" Jamal nodded while grinning. "So, do you see her often?" I asked.

"Only when she's here," he said.

As I was about to pose another question, a massive burst of laugher echoed from down the hall, where we saw Asè dancing to some hip hop music with the kids. Her moves were so funny, we couldn't help but join in the laughter.

"Bruh," Jamal said, still trying to recover from laughing. "I asked my pops one time what Asè look liked back in the day when he was younger. He told me she looked just like that." Jamal pointed his finger in Asè's direction. "But it's crazy because I probably saw her like two or three seasons in my life, and she looked the same then as she does now."

"Yeah, that's crazy, bruh. It's like she doesn't age," I said. "But what you meant by *seasons,* though?"

"Man, you know," Jamal replied. "She pops up for a

season … Usually spring or summer … Does her thang … Then dips back out for like five to ten years."

"Facts." I nodded. "So how often does she come here to the center?"

"A lot … when she's in town," he answered. "Technically, she works here."

My jaw dropped. "Are you serious? Asè has a job?"

"No. No." Jamal laughed. "Not like that. Check it," he motioned to explain. "You remember this center used to be an event building, right?" he asked while sweeping his right arm around the building. I nodded twice. "Well, when I took over some years back, pops told me to let the old woman help me run the place, so I did. And within one year, she turned it into a community center."

"Word?" I asked with my eyes wide open. "So Asè was the reason?"

"Yep. I couldn't make this up if I tried, bruh."

"Nah, I believe you … it's just …" I stepped back to process the news. "So, what does she do here?"

"That's the funny thing about it," he said. "She doesn't manage people, answer phones, work the counter, or anything. She just hangs around and talks to people." Before I could respond, Jamal continued. "But everybody loves her, though, from customers to employees. Wherever she posts up at round here, she always draws a crowd."

We both looked down the hall at Asè again, with the kids circling her. "Just like that huh?" I asked

"Yep, just like that," Jamal said. "And I don't know where

she sleeps or lives at, but whenever she shows up, she always fresh and clean with a new African dress on, smelling like—"

"Lavender," I interrupted.

"Yep, lavender … and roses," Jamal said, laughing, then smacking his hand on the counter.

Asè finally looked up in our direction, waved, and continued chatting with the youth.

"So, what days does she work?" I asked.

"She's here most weekdays but not all day," Jamal answered. "She normally pops up sometime before lunch, but I can never tell when she leaves."

"That's Asè for ya," I said sarcastically. "Always disappearing."

Jamal slumped over the counter, looking off into the distance. "You know," he turned to me, "This is the longest I think she's ever been around."

"Yeah, I've heard that too. I wonder what she's up to?"

Jamal shrugged.

ASÈ HAD JUST FINISHED HOSTING A BUSINESS workshop across the hall from the gift shop to a group of teens, who were now in the parking lot waiting for their rides. As she made her way to the back of the center near the playground, Asè noticed three of the teens who hadn't left, sitting on the picnic tables.

"Hey Asè!" the basketball star, ZaZa, said, walking

towards her. "What you still doing here?"

"I should be asking you that chile," she answered. "Shouldn't y'all be getting home?"

"We just cooling … chopping it up with Corey before he leaves to go to Clemson," ZaZa said.

"Oh, ok," Asè replied.

"I'm about to go get us some juices from the lounge before they close. You want one?" ZaZa asked.

"No, I'm fine, honey. But thank you."

"Alright den," ZaZa said as she walked inside the building.

ZaZa was a pretty tomboy with long natural braids hanging down her back. She was about 5'9, slim, and one of the most popular girls at CA Johnson High School. Many guys liked to her, yet she remained *involuntarily* single.

As Asè passed the swings walking toward the picnic tables, she glanced at Sharina, ZaZa's best friend, who was sitting on top of one. Sharina, a sophomore in college at Benedict, was two years older than ZaZa, yet still worked at Crews for the summers. She was a graphic design major following in the footsteps of her estranged father, a longtime animator for the local paper.

Sitting in the wooden chair right next to her was Corey, a handsome eighteen-year-old computer geek approaching his first year of college. He was born and raised in Liberty Heights but moved to Lexington, where the whites resided after his dad inherited insurance money from his grandfather's death. Though he stayed far away, his parents still forced him to work at the Center during summers so that he didn't forget where he came from.

"Hey Asè," Sharina said.

"What's happening, my beloveds?" she replied.

Corey put his hands up. "Nothing, just chillin."

Asè sat backward on the bench of the table behind them with her bag folded on her lap. ZaZa strolled up shortly, distributed the juices, and sat down next to Asè. With the foursome, now evenly facing each other, Asè went to work.

"So, what you guys talking about?" she asked.

Sharina and ZaZa looked at each other, smirking. Corey smiled falsely, swallowing his spit with guilt.

"Well, don't all answer at once." Asè smiled.

The silence continued, and a staring contest broke out between the four. Then, without warning, Sharina blurted out: "We were just trying to get some dating advice from Corey."

Corey shook his head, ashamed of where the convo was headed.

"Is that right?" Asè eyeballed Corey. "I didn't know you were a ladies man, son?"

He shrugged his shoulders. "Me neither."

"Well, you must be if these two beautiful young ladies are asking *you* for dating tips," she replied.

"No, it's not like that, Asè." ZaZa shook her head. "We just wanted to know why do black guys seem to prefer white girls over us?"

"Yeah, and Corey over here is an expert on that," Sharina

said, laughing out loud, as did Zaza.

Corey raised from his slouch. "C'mon y'all. How you gon play me like that in front of Asè?"

"Ohhh." Asè joined the girls with a short grin then faced Corey. "So you got jungle fever, son?"

"No," he replied. "I like all shades of women. My girlfriend right now just happens to be white."

"Yeah, right, bruh. Stop lying." ZaZa smirked.

"Yeah, why you tryna front?" Sharina tapped him on the leg. "You know you only date white girls."

Asè leaned back and folded her leg over the top of the other. "Stop messing with 'em girls. Let the man speak for himself," she said. "So, Corey. Your current girlfriend is Caucasian?"

"Yes ma'am," he said softly.

"What was your last girlfriend?" she asked.

Seeing his hesitation, Asè chimed in. "It's alright, son. You know there's no judgment over here." She then looked at ZaZa and Sharina. "At least not from me."

"Ok," he answered. "She was Caucasian."

"Oh, ok. Well, you seem a little too young to have had multiple girlfriends, but since you're a ladies man," she smiled, "I'll ask. What about the one before that?"

"Uh. She was white too," Corey said reluctantly.

ZaZa and Sharina burst out laughing. "I told you," Sharina said.

"Dang, son. That sure is a lot of vanilla for a chocolate brother," Asè laughed out loud. "If I didn't know any better,

I would think Sharina and ZaZa were telling the truth."

"Nah, I mean. It's not that I don't like black girls, it's just that … well, they don't … I just haven't found one that I like yet."

"Really?" Asè replied. "So, you telling me that out of all of the black girls you run across—none of them interest you?"

"Nah, I ain't mean it like that."

"Well, talk to me son. What did you mean?" Asè asked gently.

After much hesitation, he finally spilled the beans. "I'm just more attracted to white women. There, I said it."

Asè looked out the corner of her eyes at both girls. ZaZa folded her arms with disgust, and Sharina's eyes became heavy with sadness. She could feel their pain weeping inside her soul.

"Well, thank ya for ya honesty, son. It took ya long enough." She smiled.

Corey now felt at ease, like the weight of the world was no longer on his shoulders. "Asè, you know how it is," he said. "I just don't like how everybody be hating on me cuz I like white girls."

"Oh, trust me. Nobody's hating on you, son. If anything, people are worried."

"Worried about what?" he asked.

"I'll get to that in a few. But first, answer me this," Asè said. "What is it that you find attractive about white girls that you don't see in your sisters?"

Eager to hear his answer, Sharina almost snapped her neck to face Corey. "Damn, why you all up in my face?" he asked.

"Boy, just answer the question," she replied.

"Ok. Well, I just like how they look and carry themselves."

"What da hell you mean by that?" Sharina asked.

"Sharina!" Asè raised her voice with finesse. "You gotta let him talk if you want to hear the answer."

"Ok … ok. .. I'm sorry Asè. I'll be quiet," she replied.

"You see that right there. That's what I'm talking about." Corey said. "They don't be acting all ratchet and ghetto like that." Facing Sharina, he added, "They act like ladies."

Sharina stumped her feet on the bench and was about to respond, then looked at Asè and placed her hand over her mouth. But ZaZa held no punches. "Are you serious, Corey?" she yelled. "So, you think we ghetto?"

"No, not you," he said. "Not even Sharina. But I'm saying tho … y'all do have some ghetto ways about y'all." He laughed.

"Oh. So because you live around white folks now … how we act is ghetto. Boy bye." ZaZa shook her head with disgust.

"Well, if we so ghetto bruh—then why you like hanging with us?" Sharina asked.

"Cuz y'all my friends," he answered. Noticing both of the girls' unhappy faces, Corey leaned forward and said, "C'mon y'all. Don't make me out to be the bad guy. I'm just answering questions."

"True indeed son. So let's continue," Asè intervened.

"You also mentioned looks. So what is it about white girls that you find attractive?"

Corey leaned back on the table. "Well, I guess it's —"

"No need to guess, son. Just tell me what you like about 'em?"

"Okayyy," he said annoyingly. "I like their complexion. And the way they wear *their* hair."

The girls sat frozen, appalled at Corey's answer.

"Whew. You said a mouthful there, son." Asè gently patted his leg, then leaned back on the bench. "Can we unpack some of that?" Corey nodded reluctantly.

"So what did you mean by their complexion … the paleness of it?" she asked.

"No. I met, just having a pure skin color," he answered. "You know … like without flaws."

ZaZa clenched her fist and began and leaned forward to get up, but Asè tapped her on the back, motioning for her to relax. "Well, let me ask you this son," Asè said, staring at Corey with sternness. "What color is your mother?"

Corey raised his eyebrows. "What you mean? She's black like me."

"Indeed," Asè replied. "So, would you consider her skin color pure or flawed?"

Stunned by the question, Corey rubbed his chin, pondering an answer. After a few seconds of silence, Asè interrupted. "Well, let's move on to the next question then. You said you like how white girls wear their hair, right?" Corey nodded with guilt. "So, what is it about their hair that you like?"

"I don't know. I just like how they wear their own hair," he said, staring at Sharina's blonde wig. "You know how black girls be wearing wigs and weaves and all that stuff. But white girls just wear their hair. And I like that."

Sharina sucked her teeth and was about to speak up, but Asè interrupted again.

"What about your mama? Does she wear fake hair too?"

"Yep. All the time," Corey replied. "I can't even remember what my mom's real hair looks like."

"And why do you think that is?" Asè asked. "Why do you think so many black women wear wigs and weaves, son?"

Corey shrugged. "I don't know. I always wondered that."

"It's because of men like you," Asè proclaimed.

"Huh? What you mean by that?"

"Asè sat up straight and peered into Corey's eyes. "Well, due to the white supremacist mindset that so many brothas have been raised with, your sistas know what you guys are attracted to. They know you like white women and that *if* you do choose a sista, you want her to have European features. So they sew-in other people's hair or fry and dye their own, to get it straight and silky just the way you guys like it."

Feeling guilty as charged, Sharina finally kept quiet. ZaZa, on the other hand, spoke her peace. "Yep," she nodded. "That's the same thing my daddy say, Asè—that we alter ourselves to please them."

"Dang.," Corey said. "I never thought about it like that."

"It's alright, son. That's why we're having this conversation," Asè replied. "But to be fair, not all sistas think like this.

I know you've seen plenty of young girls round here who are perfectly fine with wearing their natural hair, or at least in a style that looks like it ..."

Corey nodded slowly.

"And since you say that's what you like," Asè smiled, "then why aren't you attracted to them?"

Unsure of an answer, Corey didn't respond. So, Asè proceeded to help him out. "Well, let's take ZaZa here, for example," she motioned to her left. "Her hair is natural, long, and beautifully braided down her back. But that's me talking," she said. "What do you think of her hair, son?"

"Uh," Corey hesitated. "It looks good. It's just ..."

"It's just what?" ZaZa asked.

"Now you know you my homie, ZaZa. So don't take this the wrong way, ok?"

"Oh, I'm good bruh," she replied. "Now answer the question."

"Yo braids look good. They just a little nappy, that's all," Corey said, laughing.

"Wow," ZaZa said. "You—"

"Wait a minute," Sharina interrupted. "But don't that lil white girl you talk to wear braids?"

"Yeah. But hers ain't nappy tho."

"Oh. So, braids look good on a white girl, but nappy on us, huh?" Sharina shook her head. "Y'all niggas a trip."

"They sho is girl," Zaza chimed in. "They love to see our culture on everyone but us. That's why they pass up on black girls for a white girl trying to look like one."

Asè nodded and smiled proudly at ZaZa, then looked over at Corey. "I have to agree with ZaZa on this, son," she said. "You ain't attracted to white girls because they're more natural than your sistas; you're attracted to them because they are NOT your sistas."

Corey put his hand on his head in amazement. This was the first time in his life he heard such an explanation for his attraction to white girls. It made so much sense, he couldn't believe it. "Man," he said shaking his head. "You might be right, Asè."

"Ain't no *might* about it," Sharina interrupted. "She is right. That's exactly why my dad left my mom."

"Really?" ZaZa asked. "That's why your parents divorced?"

"Hold on," Corey said. "I thought Mr. Mike was your dad."

"No, that's my stepdaddy. My mom left my real dad a few years ago after she caught him cheating with one of his co-workers. A white woman with dreadlocks."

ZaZa sucked her teeth. "Man, I'm so glad my daddy not brainwashed like that."

"Y'all keep mentioning brainwashed," Corey said. "What do you mean by that?" he asked, looking at Asè.

"She means that you are not in your right mind, son. And neither are many of the brothas in this community. Y'all have been *programmed* with a European psyche."

The word "programmed" triggered something in Corey's brain. "How so?" he asked.

Asè reached down and lifted the bottom of her dress off the ground. It had patterns of the shape of Africa all around it. Then she looked up at Corey and asked, "Well, son. Let me ask this. Who are you?"

"What do you mean?"

"I mean, what is your ethnicity?"

He looked at her as if it was a trick question. "I'm Black," he said.

"No, black is a color son … A color that doesn't even apply to many of us anymore," she said. "So, who are you ancestrally?" Seeing the delusion on his face, Asè gave him the answer. "You're African, son."

"Oh, I see what you're saying now," Corey said. "Ok, I'm an African … an African-American."

Asè smiled. "And how does an African think, son?" she asked. "Or better yet, what is the mindset of an African?"

Corey pondered for a few moments, then said, "I don't know."

Asè looked at him with compassion. "So if you don't know the mindset of your ancestors, then whose mindset do you have?"

"A European's?" he ventured.

"Bingo!" Asè affirmed. "But it's not just you, son. It's most of us in this community." She looked to her right at ZaZa, and then across from her at Sharina. After placing her eyes back on Corey, she said, "And do you know how we came to develop this Eurocentric mind?"

"From slavery," ZaZa answered.

"Well, that's definitely where it started, beloved," Asè said. "But that ain't where it ended." The group awaited her response with eagerness. All ears were open for her wisdom.

"You see, not all of the slaves were stripped from their culture. Some of them were able to hold on to at least portions of it and pass it down to their youngins. That was the case with y'all ancestors here in Liberty Heights. After they fought for their freedom in Georgetown, they migrated here to establish an African-centered community . . . still practicing the customs and traditions of their ancestors without missing a beat." She paused and let out a deep sigh. "But after the era of integration, everything began to change."

All of a sudden, Asè stopped talking, and sadness filled the air. Sitting next to her, ZaZa could feel the pain of Asè's soul reaping off her elbow as it rubbed against hers. Then a tear fell from her left eye, and both Corey and Sharina looked at each other with shock. This was the first time any of them had seen her give any hint of weakness. It was as if she had a connection to those specific ancestors. Then, without warning, she spoke.

"Many folks started intermingling with the children of those who enslaved us. Moving into their neighborhoods and allowing them to move into ours. Selling our land and businesses to go and work for them. Sending our children off to their schools and colleges. And after decades of learning and adopting their ways, we lost our identity and became like them."

"Ohhh," Corey yelled. "So this is what you meant by us

being brainwashed?" he reasoned. "Our minds have been washed away and replaced with European ones; the same way you alter a computer's programming by replacing it with new software?" He asked excitedly as if he had solved the answer to a crime.

"Exactly son. I knew you would get it," she teased.

"Bout time." Zaza grinned.

"Yeah, it took you long enough," Sharina added.

Asè grinned at Sharina and then faced ZaZa. "But the brainwashing didn't stop there either, chile. It continued through mainstream media."

"For decades," Asè continued, "the media outlets have promoted whiteness as the ideal standard of beauty. They did this in films, shows, commercials, ads, and everything else you consume. And since we owned very few media productions, we never got to see ourselves as beautiful. As a result, many brothers developed an attraction for white beauty standards, so our sisters started altering themselves to cater to them."

"Not me," ZaZa said. "I love myself just the way I am." Sharina looked at ZaZa enviously, wishing she had the same confidence.

Corey looked at the girls and then back at Asè. "So, is it wrong to date or marry someone outside of my race?"

"Well, you know I don't deal in rights or wrongs, son," she said. "But what I can tell you is, it's not natural. And anything un-natural is not the best option for you."

"Un-natural?" he questioned.

"Yeah, son. You remember the class I taught on nature,

right?"

He nodded. "The one about the different species of animals and how they each lived according to their genetics?"

"Yep," she replied. "You see, thoroughbred animals living in their natural habitat only mate with each other because they love themselves and want to continue their offspring. The only animals that mate with other species are those that have been domesticated or forced to; like all these mutts y'all call dogs."

"And the same goes for us," she continued. "Back in ancient Africa before we were colonized, we didn't think to marry outside of our own either. But now that we have been socialized in the ways of others, we find ourselves desiring to be with everyone but us."

"Dang," ZaZa said, in awe of the revelation she just received. "So it all goes back to our programming, huh?"

"That's right, honey. Everything we do is based on our perception. And our perception is based on our programming."

"But what about love Asè?" Corey interrupted. "You can't help who you fall in love with, right?"

She smiled with compassion. "You may be too young to fully comprehend what love means right now, son," she said. "But know this. Love is not some feeling you catch; it's a choice. And you can't truly love another until you first learn to love yourself."

"But I do love myself," he pleaded.

"Chile please."

Corey lifted his hands as if to say *I'm serious.*

"How can you love yourself," Asè asked, "if you only desire to be with women who look nothing like you?"

Corey was stumped. His mouth stood wide open for like half of minute, pondering her question. Meanwhile, Sharina and ZaZa stared at each other, nodding, finally understanding why the fellas choose white girls over them.

After Corey snapped out of it, he noticed the girls were staring at him. Feeling embarrassed, he slammed his drink on the table and looked at Asè. "So you saying I hate myself?" he asked aggressively.

"Well," Asè said, shrugging her shoulders, "You called ZaZa's hair nappy, and yet you have the same kinks. You called your mama's skin flawed, and yet your skin looks just like hers." She placed her hands on her hips. "So, if I was a betting lady, I would say the love you have for white women stems from the hate you have for yourself."

Sensing the pain in his soul, she got up and gave Corey a hug. After a short embrace between the two, she backed up and said, "Look at me, son." He looked down and into her eyes. "Now what do you see?" she asked.

Corey looked perplexed. Unsure of the question, he gave the easiest answer. "A beautiful black woman."

"Why thank ya, son. But I know that's not really what you see." She laughed. "Do you know what I see when I look at you, though?"

"No, what?" he asked.

"Myself."

Corey's eyebrows sprung up to his forehead.

"Yep. You are a reflection of me, son," Asè proclaimed. Facing Sharina, she said, "And so are you." Then, looking back, she added, "And you too, ZaZa. We are all emanations of *The All*. So when I see y'all, I see myself—because we are one. And I love you as I love myself." Then facing Corey again, she concluded, "This is the mindset of an African."

"Beep, Beep," a loud horn blew from the parking lot. The group looked back to see whose car was blowing their horn. It was ZaZa's mom, Tina Smalls, coming to pick up her and Sharina.

The two said their goodbyes to Corey, and Asè walked them to the car and had a friendly chat with Tina. After they pulled off, Asè saw Corey leaning up against his car, waiting for her.

"One last question Asè," he said, as she walked toward him. Her eyebrows lifted with anticipation. "How do you learn to love yourself?"

Asè smiled. "By embracing who you are and where you come from," she answered.

"But I don't know where I come from," he replied.

"Sure you do," she said. "You just don't remember in this lifetime."

Corey looked confused. So Asè pointed at the steel sign in front of the building next to the center. "Read that," she said. "It will refresh your memory."

Corey walked over to the sign. It was a white steel monument with black text on it that read:

FREE BLACKS OF LIBERTY HEIGHTS
Just to the west lies Liberty Heights, settled in 1811 by approximately two hundred and thirty formerly enslaved West Africans and Black Indians who received over 300 acres of land from William Hashfess, the son of a Creek Indian chief who previously owned them. The various tribes worked together as farmers, craftspeople, boatmen, teachers, healers, artists, and traders. By 1877, they were the most prosperous group of blacks in America. Liberty Heights remained a vigorous black community into 20th century.

As Corey read the sign, his genetic memory kicked in, and he somehow felt a connection to Sierra Leone. After he finished reading, he looked around for Asè, but she was gone.

SEVEN

TAMEKA RANDOLF SAW A STRANGE FIGURE dressed in all black walking through Benedict Courts underneath the train tracks. Inside one hand was a small steel toolbox, and in the other, a red gas can. Their face was covered, blending in with the darkness of midnight.

It's probably just the landlord or the maintenance man working late, she reasoned. But as the train jolted and screeched back into motion, Tameka saw the figure pulling off one of the hoses of the gas pipes on the side of the power building. It looked strange, so she turned all the way around, trying to catch their next move as the train drifted away. From her glasses' lenses, she saw the figure pouring gas all over the concrete next to the pipes.

All the way home, Tameka wondered who that person was and what they were doing. She worked as a temporary receptionist for the public housing office over those projects and knew many folks who lived there. Worried for their safety, Tameka thought to call her boss, but she didn't want to explain to him what she was doing out this late. Airing out a deep sigh, Tameka leaned her head against the window.

The man in the seat in front of her cursed and complained—the midnight train from Liberty Heights to Sunset always tested new riders' patience. The journey was only supposed to take about twenty-four minutes, but it rarely did, as all the trains from her station seemed to have mechanical issues. But Tameka was used to it. This was the only form of transportation she had from her night shift at the strip joint, Club LaRoice.

As Tameka patiently waited for her stop, which was now less than five minutes away, she spotted something at the Shell Gas station that caught her eye. It was a white man with blonde hair getting out of a blue truck wearing the same all-black clothes as the figure from the projects. But this time, no gloves or face mask.

"That's him," she yelled. The remaining passengers look back at her like what the hell is this girl talking about. She placed her hand on her mouth, embarrassed. *That was him*, she whispered to herself, as the gas station faded into the distance.

"It sure is, honey," a voice uttered two seats behind her. Tameka looked back and saw an old woman with an African dress on, waving at her with a gentle smile. "That was him," she said.

Tameka looked confused. "Oh, you saw him too?"

The old woman nodded.

"What was he doing?" asked Tameka.

"Nothing good, that's for sure," she replied.

"Yeah, I didn't think so either."

The train screeched, attempting to break as it came up on the next stop. When Tameka grabbed her belongings and stood up to exit, the old woman spoke out from her seat, "Don't forget what you saw, baby. Your testimony may be needed in the future."

Tameka's eyebrows raised. She stared curiously at the old woman as she walked off the train. After walking past the empty seats on Columbia College Drive, she looked up to where the old woman was sitting. But no one was there.

ON THE FOLLOWING MORNING, GILBERT SUELL enters the kitchen to fry some eggs for him, his wife Wanda, and their five-year-old daughter, Mariah.

"I want some too, pops," his spoiled twenty-year-old son, Matthew, yells from the couch in front of the TV.

"Yo legs ain't broke boy," Gilbert replied. "Get yo ass in here and make your own."

Matthew sucked his teeth as he stomped toward the kitchen.

"Boy, you betta calm yo ass down before I drop you like a bad habit. Now here," Gilbert said, handing Matthew the spatula. "Finish scrambling these." He motioned towards the remaining eggs in the pan.

As Gilbert walks to the dinner table, he sees his wife Wanda shaking her head at him for always being so hard on their only son. "What?" He shrugs. But she doesn't respond.

After Matthew finished his eggs, he scooped up some grits and sat down at the table with the rest of the family. Gilbert, Wanda, and Mariah talked about what they were going to do today as Matthew scrolled through his phone. "Oh, snap," Matthew shouted. "Yo, mama, check this out. They forcing everybody in BC to evacuate their homes."

"What you talking about, Matt? Where you see that at?" Wanda asked.

"It's all over Facebook, ma. Everybody's reposting about it."

Gilbert swallowed his food with quickness, almost choking as he pulled out his phone and opened up the Facebook app, where he immediately saw the news on his timeline. The headlines read: *2 Died This Morning At Benedict Courts And Residents Are Forced to Evacuate!*

"Oh shit," Gilbert said.

He clicked on one of the articles to read more about it. Wanda leaned in closer to read along as well. As Gilbert skimmed through the story, he saw the testimonies of the residents who blamed him for the gas leaks. "Here we go again." He shook his head. "I'm so tired of this shit," he yelled, slamming his fist on the table.

"What's wrong daddy?" Mariah asked.

"Nothing baby. I'm alright."

Shaking his head, he looked over at Matthew with disgust

and told him he needed to get a job or end up like the people in Benedict Courts. Then Gilbert got up from the table and went to his room. Wanda followed him.

Gilbert sat on the edge of his bed, riddled with anger. "These lowlives getting on my nerves," he said to Wanda, "Always blaming me for something they caused."

"Stop calling them that," Wanda said. "We used to live there too. So what does that make us?"

With his face beaming red off his high yellow skin, Gilbert paid his wife no mind. After he finished reading the article, he noticed some missed texts from his co-workers and board members. Most were links to articles about the same story. But one of them was a link to a YouTube video that Channel 5 FOX News had just uploaded. He clicked on the YouTube link to hear their report:

Yesterday, gas leaks were discovered in dozens of apartments in Allen Benedict Courts Housing. Some of them with "severe and lethal" levels of carbon monoxide detected by the Columbia fire department after two men were found dead in separate apartments. This morning, Richland County Coroner Terry Watts confirmed that both men died of carbon monoxide poisoning. Subsequently, over 400 Benedict Court residents have been ousted from their apartments, officials say. Residents are being temporarily housed at local hotels.

This story is one of a continuing series covering the public housing crisis in Columbia. Just a few months ago, a similar gas leak broke out in Gonzalez Gardens, forcing those residents to evacuate as well. As a result, Benedict Court, built in the 1930s, is set to be torn down just like Columbia's other public-housing projects. City Councilman, Jesse Thompson, has called for the resignation of Housing Authority director Gilbert Suell in the wake of another gas leak. We hope to hear from Mr. Suell later this evening.

Gilbert threw his phone across the room. "Fuck," he yelled. He got up from the bed and began pacing across the room. "You at it again, huh, Jesse?" he said to himself. "Well, you couldn't get rid of me then. And you ain't getting rid of me now!"

"Baby, calm down."

Breathing heavy, as if he had just finished a race, he ran across the room to pick up his cell phone off the floor. He thought to call his publicist but noticed a missed voicemail from his longtime friend and the city's chief zoning officer, Rodney Jenkins. After listening to his message, he called right back.

"Hey Rod."

"Hey man, I know you heard the news, right?"

"Yeah man, they after me again," he replied. "And Jesse punk ass still trying to take me down."

"Yeah I see," said Rodney. "But don't worry about that, Gib. I got it all under control."

"How?"

"I found some new developers who want to purchase the land where BC is at."

"Really? Damn, you don't be playing Rodney. That's was fast as hell."

"Yeah, man. So all you have to do is get on the air tonight and convince the public that it was the resident's fault. That way, the city will seek to do something else with it, rather than rebuilding it for them."

"It is their fault as far as I'm concerned," Gilbert replied. "They always fucking up something in the building and then looking around at us to fix it."

"Yeah, I know right," Jenkins laughed. "Well, good deal Gib. Go ahead and reach out to the station so you can go on air tonight. You already know they're waiting to hear from you."

"Yep. And I'm a give 'em what they want too."

They both laughed and agreed to catch up later.

Gilbert didn't waste any time. He immediately called the news station. Wanda pressed him for answers, but he waved her off. The station requested him to come down to the projects before 6, so they could interview him live for the evening news. He did, and he gave them the most controversial speech of the year.

He called the residents a bunch of hoodlums and low lives and blamed them for tearing up the pipes. "They shoot up and kill each other every night and then act like it's the worst thing in the world for two more to die from the gas leaks that they probably caused. So if you ask me," Gilbert said to the reporter, "I think it's time for BC to be shut down for good so this land can be put to better use."

The residents who were kicked out of their homes came back to hear his speech. They were standing behind him and infuriated by his words. Insults and threats poured out from the crowd. But some people just wanted to be heard.

"Aye lady," a woman yelled at the reporter, with her infant son in her arms. "Point yo camera over here."

The reporter turned around, and her camera-men panned to the mother. "Mr. Suell is a liar," she said. "We've been complaining about these random gas leaks and pipes for months, and nobody came to do anything about it. They don't ever do nothing for us. Nobody cares whether we die or live." She cried.

"That's because y'all don't care," Gilbert replied with sarcasm.

A frenzy broke out. Everybody started yelling and cursing, and three men ran towards Gilbert, trying to attack him. But they were all hemmed up by the policeman on duty.

"You see this?" Gilbert said to the reporter. "This is why this place needs to be shut down."

GILBERT PULLED INTO HIS PARKING SPACE AT The Public Housing Office on Monday morning. As he got out of the car and walked towards the entrance door, he noticed a beautiful old woman around his age sitting on the bench outside. She smiled at him, got out of her seat, and said, "Hey Mr. Suell, you got a moment, sir?"

Damn, this lady is fine, he thought to himself. "Hey. Do I know you, ma'am?"

"No, but I know you," she replied. Then she reached out her hand for a shake. "I'm Asè."

He squelched his face with curiosity as he shook her hand. "Oh, you're the mystery woman that everybody's been rambling about?"

"That'd be me, sir."

"I figured you would have a cape on or something, the way these folks talk about you." He grinned.

"Oh, no. I'm as regular as it gets."

"I doubt that," he replied. "Well, Miss Asè, I have—"

"No Miss's sir," she interrupted. "Just Asè."

"Ok. Well, Ah-shay," he pronounced slowly, "I have to get inside the office. Is there anything I can help you with?"

"No, I'm fine sir, but there is something that I would like to help you with."

"Oh yeah. What's that?"

"I want to help you right the wrongs you have done to the folks at BC."

"Excuse me, lady?"

She held her speech as a lady walked by to go inside the office. Gilbert greeted the woman and held the door open for her.

"Yeah. You falsely accused the residents of starting those gas leaks."

"Ma'am. I don't have time for this. I have to go." He grabbed the handle to re-open the door.

"Well, I know who did it, and the truth will be out soon enough."

Gilbert stopped in his tracks, let the handle go, and turned around slowly towards Asè. She smiled and took a step closer to him. "I just thought I'd come by and give you a chance to keep it real with me before it's too late."

Gilbert sighed, tightening his lips with anger. "Come inside," he said. "Follow me to my office."

Asè walked alongside Gilbert while he greeted the folks at the front desk. As they walked past the lobby, his receptionist Tameka noticed the old woman from the midnight train a few days prior. Asè winked at her and waved. Tameka put her hand up slowly, amazed to see the old woman again.

Gilbert closed his office door and motioned for the old woman to have a seat. Then he strolled around behind his desk to do the same.

"Alright. What's your angle lady? What do you want from me?"

"I don't want from you chile, I want for you," Asè replied. She moved her bag from her lap and placed it on the floor. "Like I told ya outside … I just want to help you redeem yourself from blaming those gas leaks on the residents."

Gilbert placed his fingers together on top of his desk and looked the lady firmly in her eyes. "Do you really know who started the gas leaks, or you just pulling my leg?"

"Oh no, I wouldn't dare do that to ya, Gilbert. That would make you a cripple."

"A cripple?" He asked. "What you talking about, lady?"

"Well, your buddy Mr. Jenkins already pulling one of yo legs," she replied. "If I pulled the other, you wouldn't be able to walk." Her mouth sounded with uncontrollable laughter as she patted her right thigh. But Gilbert didn't find her funny.

"How you know Jenkins?" he asked. "And what you mean, he pulling my leg?"

"How I know him ain't important. Only why I know him is," Asè replied. "But your friend is using you now just like he used you back in high school."

Gilbert's mouth opened wide as a pothole. "Wait a minute now. How do you know all of this? Did you go to C.A. Johnson with us or something?" He asked.

"Nope." She grinned. "I'm a Perceptionist."

"A what?" he asked.

"A Perceptionist," she repeated. "I'm able to perceive things about the past and the present, which enables me to create a better future. It's my gift."

"Whoa. This is too much," Gilbert said, leaning back in his chair. "So you saying that you perceived our friendship from over thirty years ago, without even being there?"

"Well, I never said I wasn't there," she replied. "But yeah, something like that."

Gilbert placed his hands over his chin, trying to take it all in. "So you know about the things Rodney used to get me to do for him back at Johnson?" he grinned with shame.

"Yep," she answered. "Stealing the teacher's candy for him to sell at lunch. Forging his name on the Honor roll list. Etcetera, etcetera."

"My goodness." Gilbert's eyes widened. "You really do have a gift."

"Hm-mm," she responded. "So tell me something Gib … Why did you allow Rodney to use you like that when y'all were young?"

"Well," he pondered, "back in those days, I wasn't the man like I am today." He grabbed the collars on his suit jacket with full confidence. "We had just moved to Liberty Heights when I started going to Johnson. And being the new kid on the block, I had trouble finding friends. I was constantly picked on for my holey pants and knock off shoes," he laughed. "Rodney was like the only cat who would talk to me. So we became friends."

"But," Gilbert continued, "I knew Rodney was always up to no good. And I didn't like how I was always the one he chose to carry out his schemes," he sighed. "But hey—it beat being alone. Because at Johnson in the '70s … the last thing you wanted to be was alone. You know?"

"Oooh yeah, chile," Asè replied. "I heard Johnson was like 'Lean On Me' back in those days." She laughed out loud. And so did Gilbert. "But you ever asked yourself, why did Rodney choose to befriend you when no one else would?"

Gilbert looked dumbfounded. "No, I actually never thought about that," he said. "You don't think about those types of things when you're young."

"Indeed," Asè replied. "Well, have you thought about it recently?" she asked. "Because the same reason he befriended you in high school is the same reason he's your friend today."

"And why is that?"

"You tell me, Gilbert," she said. "What business deal

does Rodney have you working on for him right now?"

Raising his head, he stared at the old woman, wondering how much she knew. "Well, just like you heard on the news, we're trying to shut Benedict Courts down. We want to build a sky rise on the land so that only people who can afford it can live there. That way, we don't have to keep dealing with all these bogus complaints."

"You keep saying *we*," Asè said. "But was it your idea to go to the news or his?"

Gilbert fiddled with his fingers, pondering the answer. "I guess it was Rodney's," he answered.

"No need to guess Gib—It was."

"So, what are you trying to say?"

"Well, let me ask ya one last question, and then you will see," she said. Gilbert reclined back and motioned for her to continue. "What's your relationship with Jesse Thompson?" she asked. I saw on the news he wants you fired."

"I hate him," he said. "He's been making my life a living hell since high school."

"Hmm," Asè uttered while thinking. "But ain't Jesse friends with Rodney?"

Gilbert's eyes grew tight as if he was in deep thought. But before he could answer, the old woman continued. "Now, I ain't the brightest fish in the pond, but it seems pretty strange for Rodney to send you to the news to shut down the projects after his other friend recommended to have you fired."

Gilbert froze up like a deer in headlights. "Well, I'll be damn," he said. He then started laughing and shaking his head simultaneously. "That fool played me again."

"Again?" she asked.

"Yeah," he said, shaking his head. "Rodney pulled this same stunt on me in high school. He had Jesse spread rumors about this car I was saving up to buy so that I wouldn't get it. A few months later, his parents bought it for him for graduation."

Asè started laughing. "Once a scammer; always a scammer."

Gilbert was heated. His face was bloodshot red. Then, remembering what Asè had told him outside, he replied, "You said you know who caused the gas leak ... Was it Rodney?"

"C'mon now." She placed her hands on her hips. "You know Rodney too smooth to get his hands dirty." Gilbert nodded with a slight grin, knowing she was right. "It was one of his investors," she answered.

"Investors?" His head twitched. "What you talking about, Asè?"

"Well, your best friend has been cutting deals with private investors and developers behind your back, allowing them access to set up businesses and buildings in Liberty Heights for money under the table." Leaning forward in her chair, she added, "And they are the ones causing all these gas leaks and fires 'round here."

Gilbert's jaw dropped. "Are you serious?"

"Yeah. The proof is all around you," she answered. "How else you think all these white folks and immigrants been able to move out here into an all-black community and start businesses?" she asked. "They sho' ain't get permission from the people who live out here."

"I can't believe this shit," Gilbert said. "So he been using me this whole time as his voice to the public so he could get these projects and businesses shut down … and let outsiders move in?" he questioned out loud.

"Right on," Asè confirmed. "And because you are so traumatized from your childhood experiences, Rodney was able to easily convince you that it was residents causing these issues, rather than his investors."

Gilbert got up to stretch, then walked back and forth behind his desk. "This sucka done played me long enough," he said. Then, he stopped in mid-stride, turned towards Asè, and asked, "Who created the gas leaks? You said you saw who did it, right?"

"No. I said I *know* who did it," Asè responded. "But the person who *saw* it works right here in your office?" She smiled.

His eyebrows raised. "Really?" he shouted. "Who?"

She stood up from her chair and said, "Well, before I give up that information, I need you to promise to make things right with the residents who were kicked out of their homes."

"Ughh," Gilbert blew his breath. "Why do you even care about those folks? They ain't nothing but lowlifes seeking for handouts."

"Lowlifes?" she questioned. "Those are some strong words from someone who came from those same projects."

"Yeah, but I was different. And as soon as I could, I got

out of that hellhole."

Asè reached down and picked up the small flower pot on his desk. She raised the purple rose to her nose and breathed in its aroma. Then she lowered the flower and looked up at Gilbert. "When a flower does not bloom, do you change the flower or the environment?"

Gilbert looked confused. "Huh?"

"Just answer the question."

"Ok." Looking at the flower pot, he said, "I change the soil."

"Exactly," she said. "You see, you went off to college to experience a more nurturing environment, and it made you the man you are today. That's the only thing that separates you from the folks you call lowlifes." Then she leaned over his desk and handed him the pot. "So I wanna place them in a better environment. And you gon help me give it to them."

Over the next few minutes, Asè negotiated with Gilbert to give the homeless residents the vacant land on Rosewood, a few blocks away. Unbeknown to him, their ancestors lived and farmed on the same land before Hurricane Hugo destroyed their properties and forced them into public housing. Unsure of what they would do with the land, Gilbert was just happy at the chance to finally have them out of his hair. So he agreed.

"You have my word," he said. "Now, who is the witness?"

Asè smiled and said, "It's your receptionist."

His mouthed opened wide. "Tameka?"

"Yep."

He folded his lips to the side, disappointedly. "Are you sure it was her?"

"Yes Gilbert!"

"Man," he sighed, "I was just about to fire her."

"Fire her … Why?" Asè asked.

"Because I recently found out she was a stripper," he answered. "She just doesn't know that I know."

Asè shook her head. "There you go, judging people again," she said. "You know, you bet not ever make a mistake … the way you be condemning folk."

"I hear you Asè," he said, "But c'mon now … A stripper?"

"Well, why you think the girl stripping Gilbert?" she asked. "I mean, she's a single mother of two for God's sake … how else she's supposed to take care of her kids?"

Gilbert sucked his teeth and turned his chair to the side. He wasn't trying to hear it. But Asè continued. "Maybe if you would hire her full-time, she wouldn't have to work the poles at nights."

"That's a big *maybe*."

"No, it's actually a fact," she said. "You just don't have the discernment to see it right now."

"Well, not everybody can see the future like you."

"I don't see the future; I see the now," she replied. "My view is just larger than yours because I'm not tainted by judgment. So I'm able to see the brilliance inside Tameka instead of her flaws."

Gilbert sat down quietly, processing what she had just

said. The silence let Asè know that she had won him over, so she told Gilbert it was time for her to go. He thanked her for coming and said to send Tameka to his office on her way out of the building.

"Nurture her like you do that flower, Gilbert, and she'll become your most valuable employee," Asè said as she opened the door to leave. "Trust me, I know."

EIGHT

MY TWO LITTLE ONES HOPPED ON THE COUCH and climbed on top of me. My daughter Sanaa spoke first. "I like Mrs. Asè daddy … she was nice."

"She sure is, ain't it?" I responded. "But she ain't a Miss's baby girl. So you can just call her Asè."

My wife laughed out loud from the kitchen. "You sound just like her," she said.

Asè had just left our house about fifteen minutes ago. She spent the evening with Lashonda, the kids, and me. We had such a great time, we practically begged her to stay. But she claimed to have an appointment that she had to keep. And, as always, she declined my offer to give her a ride.

"I like her too, daddy," my son Omari said. "Look what she gave me." He held up a wooden action figure of an African tribal warrior.

"This is cool, O," I replied, as I checked it out. "It looks like it came from ancient Africa."

"It did, daddy," Sanaa interrupted. "Asè said it came from Nigeria." Then, she held up a copper-made doll of Queen Nefertiti. "And mines … she said came from a place called Kemet."

"I didn't see her with any toys," I said. "When did she give these to y'all?"

"Uhhh," Omari pondered, "I think it was when you were outside checking the mail, dad."

"Yeah dad," Sanaa said. "She pulled it out of that brown bag she was carrying."

I laughed. "Ya know," I said, "she gave me my first gift from the same bag." They both looked at me with gooey eyes.

"Really? What did she give you, daddy?" Omari asked.

"Books," I answered.

I was beyond thankful that my family was finally able to meet the woman who had transformed my life. We had been in town for almost four weeks now, and I was becoming worried that they might not get to meet her. After all, I had only spent a handful of times with her myself—and they were all random. Then, surprising me yet again, there was the puppy incident …

I GOT UP AROUND SIX THE NEXT MORNING TO grab the Melanin Metro newspaper from my yard. I did this every Saturday to give me time to read it before the kids woke me up. As I opened the front door and walked onto the porch, I saw a grayish-blue puppy at the end of my driveway, seemingly barking at someone by the trees. I looked to my right and saw an old brown leather duffle bag leaning against the opposite side of the oak tree.

As I walked closer to the end of the driveway looking by the trees for you-know-who, I heard a voice from the opposite direction say, "Hey son." And there she was sitting on top of the black Cutlass I used to drive when we first met. She smiled broadly with the glow of an angel. "Do you think they will like her?"

"They who?" I asked.

"The little ones." Asè laughed. "You think they will like her?"

"Oh, you bought this dog for them?" I shook my head. "You didn't have to do that, Asè. How much did you pay for this?" I asked.

"Chile boo," she said, waving her hand away at me. "How you gon ask me a question and you ain't even answer mines yet."

I looked at the dog again. "I guess so."

She put her hand on her hips and poked out her lips. She didn't utter a word, but I could feel her vibration saying, *no guessing, son.*

"Okay, they probably will," I responded.

"Sure, they will. They've been asking you for a puppy for years now," Asè said with surety.

My face mushed up with surprise. "How did you know that?"

"Sanaa told me," she said. "And you know the kids tell it

like it is."

I laughed. "Yeah, they have been asking me to buy them a dog for a minute now. I just don't have the time for all that."

"Well then, she said. "I'm glad to be of service to ya son. They gon love Badu." Then she snapped her fingers, and the puppy immediately ran over and jumped into her arms.

I stared Asè into her eyes with anger as she rubbed the fur on her back. "Why did you buy them this dog, Asè? And how much did it cost?" I asked firmly.

"It don't matter how much it cost. They wanted one, and since you never have the time to get them one—I did."

I took a slow breath, holding back my rage. "Asè I love ya to death. But with all due respect, you messing up the way I'm parenting," I said. "I'm trying to teach my kids that they can't have everything they want."

"Why would you teach them a lie like that, son?"

My eyebrows lowered. "What you mean?" I asked. "That ain't no lie. That's the truth."

"No, that's *your* truth, son. Not *the* truth."

Calmly, she hopped off the trunk of my car and stood next to me. I looked away from her, but she grabbed my hand to draw my attention. "You teach your children that they can't have everything they want, only because you don't believe that you can have everything you want. But it's not like they asking you to buy them a car." She grinned, "All they want is a dog."

"Yeah, but that's another mouth to feed. And I already got too much on my plate as it is."

"Ahhh. So there it is," Asè said.

"There, what is?" I asked.

"The real reason you don't want a dog," she smiled.

Asè then kneeled to let the dog roam freely. After a few seconds of watching the dog play in the grass, she glanced my way. "Those money blocks you have are keeping you broke, son."

"What you talking bout now, Asè?"

"Well, son," she began, "The last time we chatted seriously, we discovered why your career wasn't progressing. But we didn't get to address why you're finances aren't."

I glanced her way, patiently awaiting her response. "Have you ever asked yourself why money seems to fly away from you, no matter how much you make?" she asked.

I laughed out loud. "Ha-ha," I said. "But yeah ... all the time."

"And?" she asked.

"I don't know Asè. It's just always been like that," I answered. "Even back in the day when I was hustling ... I was making like two stacks a week but never had much to show for it."

"Well, how bout ya, dad?" She asked. "How was he with money?"

"Not good," I replied. "Even worse than me." We both laughed.

I shared with Asè the lessons my dad taught me about rich people growing up. "They some greedy ass bastards," he used to say. "You should have just enough to get by. Any more than that, and you're just like the white man."

Asè laughed. "Well, no wonder you stay broke, son," she responded. "You were programmed to be."

"Because of that?" I shook my head. "Hell nah, I ain't like pops. I'm a go-getter. Plus, I made way more money than him." I lifted myself off the car.

"Yeah, but you don't know how to keep it," she said. "And neither did he."

"True," I said, looking at the dog running around in my yard.

"You see, son," she said as she took a few steps in front of me. "The most vital part of a person's life is their childhood. And what parents tell their children about money, usually stick with them for the rest of their life."

"So you think what my dad said stuck with me all these years?"

"You remembered it, didn't you?"

"Wow." The lightbulb was finally going off in my head.

She nodded at me, perceiving my thoughts. "Now, of course, he didn't mean to," she said. "But your dad did indeed train you to associate becoming rich with being like the white man. And nobody wants to be that right?"

I shook my head. "Nope."

"Right," she said. "So, unconsciously, you always find a way to get rid of all the extra money you make beyond just getting by; to avoid being like the white man."

"Oh my god," I shouted, falling back on the car, completely blown away. "Damn Asè, I really do have … what you call it ... Money blocks?"

"Yes. And you most definitely do." she laughed out loud. "But just like a computer," she pointed at her head, "this virus in your head can be removed. You just have to train your mind to feel accepting and deserving of abundance."

Before she left, she placed Badu in my arms and handed me three books from her bag. They were: *Think and Grow Rich*, *As A Black Man Thinketh,* and *Rev. Ike's Secrets For Health, Joy and Prosperity*.

After scanning over the covers, I looked at her walking away and sprinted forward. "I guess I'm never done learning, huh?"

She turned around and said, "Not unless you wanna stay broke." Then she smiled at me so brightly as if she was the sun herself. "But even that is a matter of perception."

Filled with joy from our convo, I watched her walked down the street before fading into the distance. Then I went back inside to show the kids their new puppy. They were so excited, they jumped on me, grabbing my legs to give me hugs. Even my wife jumped in. Then Sanaa and Omari fought over who could hold the puppy, something they still do to this day.

Although I appreciated Asè, I often wondered what made me so special that she would keep rescuing me from my ignorance. But around that time, I had begun hearing more and more stories from folks who had similar experiences with her as me, so I quickly learned that I was just one of many. She was making a name for herself this time around.

Due to her growing fame, anywhere she appeared in the

hood, a crowd would gather to ask her questions and listen attentively to her answers. Her street lectures were like scenes from the gospels, only she was a woman. And everyone who had the privilege of picking her brain emerged with a new perception of their situation.

In the evening, I drove down Rosewood and passed a huge sign at the edge of an enormous vacant land lot. The new keepers had placed a quote from Asè there for the future residents to see. She had spoken those words to a group of people staying at the Super 8 Motel after being kicked out of their homes in BC last week. They had been reciting the quote so much that it became a slogan. Looking up and seeing her words on the sign made me feel like a proud son. It read:

The home you desire to live in, build it. The neighbor you desire to have, be it. The food you desire to eat, grow it. The land is rich, but you have to produce what you desire to see.

-Asè

Word spread about her even more after Jamal's community meeting last weekend. When folks started complaining to him about what white people were doing to the town, she stood up and said, "The only power white folks have over you is the power you give them. If y'all would just stop patronizing everyone else's businesses before your own, we wouldn't even be having this meeting tonight." Many laughed, I heard, but no one argued back.

Asè had a way with words and people that was simply

divine. She could go into any venue and tell folks the truth, and they would accept what she said—after some resistance, of course—no matter how bad it hurt. Even the most distressed souls seemed to heal in her presence.

SHERRI CARTER SAT IN HER ROCKING CHAIR ON the porch, sadly looking off into the distance while the kids from the neighborhood played football in the street. Minutes later, the ball landed in her yard, snapping her out of misery, and a broad smile stretched across her face as one of the young boys ran over to grab the ball. He was wearing a black t-shirt featuring the name of my movie, *It Takes A Village*. But as the young man walked away, so did Sherri's smile.

It was late Sunday morning, and every other driveway in the neighborhood was empty from families being at church. For the past forty-plus years, Sherri had also spent her Sundays in the pews. But after her longtime pastor began preaching something new, coupled with the distress of being forced out of her home in BC, she began questioning her faith. And hadn't been to church since.

However, having the last few Sundays to herself gave Sherri time to reflect on life and the choices she made, which led to her current state—a lonely middle-aged derelict full of regrets.

"Brrring, Brrring," the phone sounded from inside. Sherri jumped up from the bench and hurried inside, down the hall of the shotgun home to the kitchen. On the phone was her brother-in-law and landlord, Mike Lawson. After a minute or two of talking, Sherri shook her head in disbelief. "Ah c'mon Mike, don't do this to me now. This the only place I got to stay."

Sherri paced back and forth, totally disoriented. "I told you those motel vouchers was only for two weeks," she shouted. "And that's right around the corner."

After hearing Mike's response, Sherri became exasperated. "No," she yelled. "I can't stay with y'all. You know your wife hates me." She drops her head while rubbing her hand over her eyes. "Well, can't you at least give me until August?" The answer must have been *no* by the way she slammed the phone into the wall.

Sherri spent the next few minutes with her head rolled over the kitchen counter, weeping. When she finally managed to lift herself up, she caught a glimpse of something through the window that immediately stopped her tears. Walking over to the sink window, she saw a woman in her backyard pruning some flowers.

"Excuse me," Sherri yelled out lightly as she stepped onto the cemented porch and headed toward the garden area. "Hey. Are you lost, Miss?" Ignoring the question, the mysterious woman took one last snipe and added the flower to the rest inside her balled-up fist. Then she opened her brown leather bag and pulled out a wooden vase to place them in.

Sherri now stood about three feet away from the older woman. "Uhhh … excuse me, ma'am," she said sarcastically. "What are you doing in my yard?"

"Hey there," the woman said, looking up with a smile. "You seem to be mistaken, beloved. This is Baba Kambon's yard. She pointed to stones in the grass separating the yards. "Your yard is right there."

Sherri glanced around, then folded her lip, realizing she was right.

"Oh. I'm sorry ma'am," she sighed. "I left my glasses in the house. You know when you get this old," she laughed, "your sight just leaves you."

Asè smiled but refused to affirm her statement. "Well, that's why I'm here, dear … to help you see again."

Sherri's eyes shrunk. "Help me see what … again?"

"The beauty of your future," Asè answered, as she stepped forward to hand her the vase. "Here. These are for you."

Sherri had been so focused on the mysterious woman that she hadn't realized the flowers she was tending were her favorite—lavender. Her father used to pick her lavender flowers from the backyard as a child. He would tell her that just as the lavender grows despite the weather, that she could achieve anything she wanted despite their circumstances. And she believed him.

Holding the vase in her hand, Sherri breathed in the smell of the flowers and smiled. "Wow," she said. "I haven't smelled one of these in years."

"Yeah, I love lavenders too," Asè replied. "They help you relax long enough to appreciate what you already have … and that's usually all we need to create the future we desire."

Sherri lowered the flowers down from her nose and stared at the woman for a few seconds. *That's something my dad used to say*, she thought. Then, out of nowhere, she said, "Who are you? Are you a friend of Baba's?" She pointed toward his front yard, where Baba was chatting with his vibrant younger brother Tommy, who had recently moved in with him.

"I am," the old woman answered, looking back at the two brothers. "And my name is Asè."

Sherri's eyebrows raised to the sky. "Really?" she stared even harder. "So you're the one everybody's around here talking about?"

Asè grinned. "You seemed surprised. Did they describe me as a man? I hate when they do that," she laughed.

"No. No," Sherri couldn't help but laugh as well. "It's just that ... I thought you'd be much older."

"Asè smiled widely. "Well, age is a matter of perception. The older you feel, the older you look."

Sherri took a moment to digest her words and then asked, "So what did you mean about me seeing beauty in my future?"

Asè looked around the yard. "How about we go have a seat over there," she pointed at the patio, "to discuss this matter, Mrs. Carter."

"Sure." As the two made their way toward the patio, Sherri realized something. "Wait. How you know my name?"

"I know everyone around here. That's my job."

Sherri placed her vase on the glass table in front of the lawn chairs and then took a seat next to Asè. "You know,"

Sherri said, "I heard about the land you arranged for us to have over there on Rosewood to build a new community. I think that's amazing." Then, pointing at her chest, she asked, "But what are old folks like me supposed to do in the meantime?"

"Why do you talk like that, Sherri? You make growing old sound like a death wish."

"It is," Sherri shouted. She then glanced at herself through the glass table. "Look at me," she said. "I'm 54 years old. Divorced. Widowed. And on the verge of being homeless. It's like I'm living to die." She sighed.

"Wow beloved," Asè uttered. "Your perception is worse than I thought." She leaned forward and placed her hand on top of Sherri's. "Let's go ahead and get started."

"Get started doing what?"

"Opening your eyes … because you obviously can't see."

Sherri folded her arms. "Oh really? So what am I missing?"

"The dreams you once had when you were a child," she answered. Stunned, Sherri leaned back in the chair and faced Asè as she continued.

"When we're children, we dream big. We know what we want and believe that we can achieve it. But then we grow older and allow others to convince us otherwise. And too often, we feel like once we pass fifty, our best years are behind us." Sherri bobbed her head repeatedly. "But that's not true," Asè said. "Usually, our worst years are behind us."

"Huh?" Sherri said in disbelief. "How so?"

"Because those are the years we make the most mistakes," she answered. "You see, life is one big learning experience. And due to being disconnected from our culture and elders, we spend the first half of our lives learning through trial and error … often failing miserably in the process."

"But," Asè continued, "By the time we're around what y'all call middle age, we are wise enough to no longer care what others think. And we have amassed an abundance of knowledge that we can use to spend the rest of our years living our best life."

As Sherri was nodding her head with hope, doubt crept in. "Yeah, right," she said with the poot face. "Who you know living their best life after fifty?"

"Woo chile. You sho are one tough egg to crack," Asè teased. "But, there are plenty," she answered.

"Well name one, then."

"I'll do ya one better. I'll name three," Asè said. Ever heard of Mignon Francois?" she asked. Sherri shook her head. "Well, Mignon is a millionaire today. But when I met her, she was broke and miserable just like you," she said playfully. "Sometime around age 50 though, she decided enough was enough and started selling cupcakes from her house with just $5 to her name. Ten years later, her company is now worth over $10 million, and she's living the life of her dreams."

"Really?"

"Yep. It's called the Cupcake Collection. Google her." As Sherri was scrolling through her phone with excitement, Asè continued. "But Mignon is one of many. You know Wendy Ida, right?"

Sherri looked up and said, "Yeah. The nice young lady who teaches weightlifting down there at Crews?"

"Hm-mm," Asè answered. "But believe it or not, Wendy's older than you."

"No, get out of here," Sherri said.

"Seriously. Wendy is 68."

Sherri's jaw dropped. "Are you serious?"

"Yep. But she didn't always look that good. Nor was she always that happy. Wendy was 80 pounds overweight and was more depressed than you when I first met her years ago." Asè laughed. "But she got into fitness around her 50's and now look at her … she's a Guinness book world record holder and one of the sexiest grandmothers in the world."

"Yeah, I would kill to have a body like hers."

"Me too, chile," Asè said. They both grinned. "But that's Wendy's dream. So only she could make it come true. So tell me, Sherri," Asè said, glancing at the flower on the table. "What's your dream?"

After a long pause, Sherri finally answered. "Well, ever since I was a little girl, I always wanted to be a writer. But not just any writer. I wanted my books to make a difference, ya know. I wanted them to lead people to the kingdom."

"What kingdom?"

"The kingdom of God," Sherri answered. "But now," she hesitated, "I'm not even sure if such a place exists."

"Of course, it does," Asè said. Sherri looked confused,

as she had heard all about her views on the bible from others. "Now I'm no Christian," she grinned, "but answer me this honey: Where did Christ say the kingdom of heaven is located?"

Sherri placed her hand on her chin briefly, then said, "Within."

"That's right," Asè affirmed. "So if you want to write books that lead people to the kingdom, then just teach them how to find it within themselves. "But," Asè raised her finger in the air, "in order to embody this message, you first must find the kingdom within yourself."

"And how do I do that?"

"Well, for starters, you gotta forgive," the old woman answered. "You gotta forgive yourself for your mistakes and wrongs towards others … so you can forgive others for their mistakes and wrongs towards you. From there, you'll be able to see the weeds blocking you from the kingdom. And you can pluck them out and start blooming," she pointed at the flower, "just like the lavender."

The two sat quietly for a moment until tears fell from Sherri's cheek, followed by intense boo-who crying. Asè quickly rose up and pulled out a tissue box from her bag. While Sherri wiped her face, Asè asked what was wrong. She lifted her head and stared into Asè's eyes with sorrow. "It's my son."

"For years, he tried to teach me some of the things about the bible that I'm just learning now," Sherri said. "But I refused to hear him. In fact, I condemned him to hell and kicked him out of my house."

As Sherri continued to talk, Asè seemed to have a flashback of something unpleasant. With her tightly eyes closed, her face crumpled up like paper, and her legs shook violently as if she was reliving Sherri's confession. Seconds later, Asè painfully snapped out of it, almost to tears. But Sherri didn't notice due to staring off into the distance as she spoke.

"But he never gave up on me, though," Sherri continued. "No matter how many times I rejected him, he always stayed in touch and would even send me money from time to time … without me even knowing." After her tears dried up, she looked intently at Asè, who stared back curiously. "Do you know he offered to buy me a house when he sold his first screenplay … but I told him no because it was the devil's money."

"Well, you need to ask him does that offer still stands," Asè laughed. Sherri couldn't help but laugh in return. Sitting back in her chair, Asè said, "But seriously honey. You should reach out to your son. He still loves you and would be happy to receive you back in his life. And it's plenty of room in that big ol' house of his for you to stay and work on your writing career."

Sherri looked puzzled. "Wait. You know Dane? And you've been to his house?"

"Yep, I sure do." Asè smiled. "You raised a fine young man. He's strong-willed and stubborn just like you."

Sherri laughed out loud, knowing it was true. "What about my grands? Have you met them too?"

Asè nodded humbly. Having not seen them in years, Sherri looked away with shame that a total stranger had spent more time with her only son and grandchildren than she did. Asè reached over and took Sherri's hand. "But they don't need me in their lives. They need you, their grandmother … and so does Dane."

Sherri's face brightened, shining like the sun high above her head. "Thank you, Asè. I truly appreciate that."

"No," Asè replied. "Thank you, Mrs. Carter, for the chance to spend some time under the sun for some girl talk. It means as much to me as it does to you." She then got up and told Sherri that she had to get going and gifted her with a book from her bag, called *Sacred Woman.* "Read this when you get a chance, dear. It will open your eyes."

Sherri smiled with gratitude and embraced Asè with a long departing hug. As the old woman strolled off toward the front yard, she said, "Exhale your past and breathe in your future, Sherri." Then, she looked back and added, "Your best life awaits you."

NINE

BRANDY LAWSON STOOD NEXT TO HER BOOTH with a towel in her hand, watching one of her only two customers all day, walk out the door. Then she plopped down in her chair, let out a loud sigh, and placed her elbow on the armrest to hold up her head. *How am I going to keep this shop open, lord?*

Brandy was forty-two years old and the owner of She Styles Hair Studio. She was on her second marriage to her high school sweetheart Mike, a small-time landlord whom she rarely saw and was pregnant with their first child. They were both raised in Liberty Heights but now lived in the suburbs of Lake Carolina, in a gigantic house they struggled to afford—and drove a Range Rover they were behind payments on.

In the past, Brandy could easily afford such things. She was a rock star hair stylist and had been earning well over six-figures for the last few years. But her lavish lifestyle and one too many shopping sprees had finally caught up with her. And Brandy now found herself broke and bitter and was on the cusp of losing her business and family.

Her attitude was so funky that both Mike and her daughter Sharina from a previous marriage kept their distance. And the unreachable expectations she placed on her co-workers made them hate her. But Brandy, being the go-getter that she was, forged ahead, doing all she could to maintain her lifestyle.

She took on clients at odd hours to accommodate them when other shops couldn't. She went to old folks homes to do hair for the elderly. She even taught classes occasionally at the local beauty school. However, there was nothing Brandy could do to make up for the lost ends of her former stylists.

After fifteen minutes of sulking, Brandy finally got up to grab the broom and began sweeping up her station. It was after 9:00, but she had forgotten to flip the 'open' sign over to 'closed.' As she was dumping the hair in the trash from the dustpan, the bell sounded from someone entering the salon.

She looked up and saw an old woman walking in with a duffle bag over her left shoulder.

"Hey there," Brandy said. "Can I help you?"

"I don't know, but I hope so," Asè replied, walking towards her booth in the back. She rubbed her hand through her hair. "I wanted to get my locks in the front re-twisted. You any good with that, sweetie?"

Brandy hadn't twisted hair in years, but she was desperate for income. "Yes ma'am. I can help you with that," she replied. Then she turned her chair in a circle motion and said, "Sit down. Let me see what you working with."

"Thank ya, sweetie." Asè placed her bag on the floor and took a seat.

Brandy twirled her chair around towards her and ran her fingers through the hair above her forehead. "So, you got some new growth here, I see."

"Yeah, chile. It's growing like weeds."

Brandy laughed. "Well, I can help you out with that. I'll wash it for you and then connect it with the rest of your twists, and you won't miss a beat."

"Sounds good to me, honey," Asè replied.

"Ok, well, what's your name Mrs., so I can mark you down in my book," Brandy said, pointing at her tablet on her desk shelf.

"I AM Asè. No Mrs. Just plain ol' Asè.

"Well, good to meet you, Asè," she said, reaching out her hand. "I'm Brandy."

Asè embraced her with both of her hands. "Likewise, honey. I've heard a lot about you. So it's good to finally meet you."

"Oh. Well, hopefully, it wasn't too bad." Brandy said with a fake smile as she wrote the woman's name down.

"Well, *bad* is a matter of perception," Asè answered. "What sounds like bad news to some is an opportunity for growth to others."

Brandy didn't quite get it. She also didn't care to ask. "Follow me over here to the sink, Asè, so we can wash your hair and get you started."

She spent the next forty-five minutes washing and drying the old woman's hair. It took longer than usual because Asè rejected the chemical-based treatments and requested natural ones, causing Brandy to catch an attitude and resist talking. She then brought Asè back over to her booth to oil her hair down.

While Brandy was in the middle of re-twisting her hair, Asè decided it was time to end the silence. "This a pretty nice salon you got here, Mrs. Lawson. How long you been in business?"

"About eight years," Brandy answered proudly. "But we started down the street at Pup's barbershop before expanding here a few years ago."

"Oh, ok," Asè said. "An all-in-one beauty and barbershop sounds interesting."

"Yeah, those were the good old days," Brandy said, looking outside the window reminiscing.

"Chile, you wasn't even born during the good ol' days. You, young folk swear y'all old," Asè said jokingly.

Brandy finally cracked a smile, followed by a laugh. "You know what I mean," she said.

"Yeah, I do," Asè replied. "But truth be told, all days are good, both past and present. It just depends on how you look at it, dear."

Brandy folded her lips. "Well, I don't know about all that," she said. "Because some days are for damn sho' bad.

Asè smiled. "Well, tell me about those good ol' days then. What was so good about them?"

"Everything."

Asè turned around in her chair with a sarcastic smirk on her face that read, *girl if you don't open your mouth and talk.*

Brandy put her hands up in defense. "Ok. Ok," she responded with laughter.

"Well, back then, doing hair used to be fun." She leaned back, staring out the window again. "See, Pup is my cousin. So when I got my beauty license, he told me I could do hair there. And I brought in so much money that he turned the shop's left side into a salon and let me bring in other stylists. So the shop became like a family affair," she said, smiling. "We would laugh and joke all day long. And the shop was always packed, so every day was a good day."

"That sounds like the best job ever, girl," Asè said. "Why you moved over here?"

"Well, I always wanted to have my own shop. I just didn't plan on opening it up so soon. I planned to work for Pups as long as I could to build up my clientele. But we ended up getting into it real big over some money, so I left and opened my salon here after that."

It's not good to cut ties with family over money, beloved, but that's none of my business, Asè said. "Speaking of business, though," she continued, "yours seems to be doing well. I read about you in the paper. They say you the best stylist in town. Is that right?" She asked, looking in the mirror across from her at Brandy.

"It said I was the best in the county, not just the city," Brandy answered.

"Ohhh. Well, excuse me, honey." Asè placed her hands

on her chest, grinning.

"You're excused," she laughed out loud, teasing. "But that was last year," she sighed. "Business has been slow this year."

"Really?" Asè asked. "How could business be slow for the best stylist in the *county*?"

"Well, for one, two of my best damn stylists left me and went to work at other shops. And they took all of their clients with them," she said, as she threw her hands up in the air. "So, I've been out here running round like a chicken with no head trying to pick up their slack." Placing her hands back in Asè's head, she mumbled, "Trifling ass heffas."

"Hmm," Asè said. "So, they just up and left you high and dry like that?"

"Yeah, girl. Can you believe that?"

Asè wasn't convinced. She could perceive some untruths. "They had to quit for a reason, though," the old woman said. "Did y'all have a dispute or something?"

Brandy got quiet for a few seconds. "Yeah. They were complaining about the way I treat them. Talking bout I was working them like slaves and that I kept raising the booth rent." She shook her head.

"Well, were you?"

"Uh. Yeah, but I had to," Brandy answered. "I got bills up to the ceiling, girl," she raised her hand towards the roof. "I had to refinance this building just to keep my house and car."

"Yeah, but what does that have to do with them?" Asè asked.

"Excuse me?" Brandy said as she removed her hands from the old woman's head.

Looking at Brandy through the mirror, Asè said, "Listen beloved, life ain't about you. It's about everybody. We all need each other to succeed as individuals. So, when you make things hard for others to make things easier for you—you end up where you are right now—a paycheck away from the street and an argument away from divorce."

Brandy stood still with a comb in her hand, staring back at the old woman through the mirror. "Who are you?"

"I told you, I'm Asè."

"No. I mean, how do you know so much about me?" She turned the old woman's chair around to face her directly. "You said that I'm an argument away from divorce … How did you know that?"

"Well honey," Asè began, "how we do one thing is usually how we do everything. So by knowing how you treat your co-workers, I perceived how you treated your husband wouldn't be much different."

"Wow," Brandy said. "You picked up all that from just a philosophy?"

"Not a philosophy—a fact," Asè answered, with her finger raised. "Look at it like this. Your best stylists left you over money issues, right?"

"Yep."

"Well, I bet you left Pup over the same money issues, didn't you?"

Brandy stepped back, amazed, and said, "Yeah."

Asè gave Brandy a nod to confirm her realization. "And how about your husband? Is he upset with you because you spend more time chasing money than you do with him?"

"Yes," Brandy said, shaking her head. "That's all he talks about." Then she caught herself. "Well, that's all he used to talk about. He hasn't spoken to me in weeks now. He's upset about me missing his birthday party to make a hair appointment."

Asè laughed at her greed. "You see," she pointed at Brandy, "in each of these scenarios, the common denominator is you. Your unquenchable thirst for money seems to be your Achilles' heel. And like I said, how we do one thing is how we do everything."

Brandy shook her head as if she was clearing the fog from her brain. "I get it, Asè," she said. "But what am I supposed to do?" she pleaded. "I'm in debt up to my eyeballs, and if I don't come up with the money, I will lose everything."

"Sometimes you have to lose to win, sweetie."

Brandy, looking disappointed at her words, replied, "What is that supposed to mean?"

"It means that losses build bridges to wins. But most people jump ship before reaching their victory. So," the old woman opened her palms widely, "do you wanna win?"

"Of course I do."

"Good," Asè said. "Well, answer me this: What is the prize?"

Brandy looked confused. "Are we still talking about the salon?"

"I don't know," Asè answered. "You tell me, honey."

She smiled at the cluelessness on Brandy's face, then asked, "You said you want to win, right? Brandy nodded. "Well, how can you win without a goal?" she asked. "A boxer wants to win the fight, a tennis player wants to win the match, and a runner wants to win the race. So what do you want to win?"

Brandy stood frozen for almost a minute, pondering an answer.

"Put the comb down and have a seat, beloved." Asè motioned to the chair to the left of her. "My hair is fine."

Brandy did as told and slouched back in the chair next to her and stretched out her legs. "You know," she said, "it just hit me … after all these years of trying to get rich, I don't even know what I want."

"You'd be surprised at how many people feel like you on this side of the globe," Asè said. "It's easy to lose one's purpose in this hustle and bustle society." Then she reached over and tapped Brandy's leg. "But let's see if we can help you find it."

Pointing at the large lettered wall décor above the entrance door that read SUCCESS, the old woman asked, "What picture comes to your mind when I say the word *success*?"

"Umm," Brandy started, "A big house … at least two stories. Two Luxury cars. Gucci and Chanel bags. Fine diamond rings and necklaces. A vacation home and a—"

"I see," Asè interrupted before Brandy could go any further. "So why does having these particular things mean success to you?"

"Because," Brandy said, "I grew up poor. My family ain't have squat. But I spent most of my summers with my cousins on my daddy side, and they stayed in Wildewood, where the rich people lived. They had a big house, nice cars, and wore name-brand clothes—all the things I wanted. And they would always pick on me for my hand-me-down clothes and nappy head," she said, touching her hair.

"But my aunt, she was the worst," Brandy continued. "For some reason, she hated me and my mama. She used to say, you Johnsons—that's my maiden name—are losers, and y'all ain't never gon be shit. So I don't know," she reflected, "I guess I just set out to prove them all wrong . . . that I could be successful too, ya know?"

Asè nodded. "Do you think you achieved your goal?"

"I used to think so," Brandy answered. "But I don't know anymore."

"It's ok beloved," Asè said as she stood up to grab some tissue from the shelf behind her and handed it to Brandy, whose eyes had become watery. "You're not the first person to measure your success based on the standards of others . . . and you won't be the last."

Asè sat back down, folded her leg over her lap. "So, now that we know what that type of 'success' looks like let's aim for another, ok?" Brandy bobbed her head. "Alright, well tell me this, beloved. What picture comes to your mind when you think of a 'joyful life'?"

Brandy thought carefully before responding. Then finally,

scratching the back of her head with a smile, she answered, "A happy home. Peace and love between me and Mike, my daughter Sharina, and my unborn child—it's a boy!"

"Awww." Asè beamed. "Congratulations, sweetie! Anything else?" she asked.

"Oh yeah," Brandy remembered. "And running a successful salon, again. One that makes women feel good about themselves."

"What an answer," Asè said. "Now, don't this picture of success look much better than the other one?"

"Yeah, it does," Brandy said while smiling from her soul.

"You see, dear," Asè replied. "What brings you joy will bring you success."

"Yeah, but joy, don't pay the bills," Brandy said jokingly, but serious.

"How would you know? You don't have any." Asè laughed.

Brandy creased her lips to the side. "C'mon now. That was a low blow."

"Well, am I wrong?" Receiving no reply, Asè glanced around the salon and then at Brandy. "I know you don't want to hear this, but I'm a tell you straight up beloved. The reason this place is empty is because of you. Your craving for more money turned you into a miserable overbearing Grinch … running everybody away. So you ain't gon start seeing mo butts back in these seats until you change your attitude."

Brandy listened carefully as if she was a little girl being disciplined by her mother.

"If you want to create a shop that makes sisters feel good about themselves, Asè continued, "You have to first feel good about yourself. That joy you felt thinking about your family," she said, "that is what you're missing. Perhaps if you spent some time with them instead of chasing money all day, you would have the joy you need to express back to others."

Brandy sat quietly for a couple of minutes, inwardly observing the crossroads her life had just reached. The old woman patiently waited and watched, giving her time to think. Looking up at the mirror in front of her booth, Brandy groaned. "I'm a hot mess, ain't it?"

"Yes, you are," Asè teased. "But only up to now."

She quickly turned to Asè. "What do you mean?"

"That YOU have the power to change," she answered. "The same way you revise people's hair, you can revise your attitude with those you love, serve, and work with. Right now, though—not as long as it takes for a hair session."

Brandy laughed and then said, "Ok then. I will change."

Asè reached over and slapped her a five. "There ya go, girl." Leaning back in her chair, she gave a friendly warning. "But just remember, you have made quite a reputation for yourself this year. So it might take a while for the "new you" to catch up with your rep. Ya dig?"

Brandy nodded. "Yes ma'am."

"Good."

As the old woman was getting out of her chair, Brandy asked, "So what can I do to show people I've changed?"

Asè pointed at her cell phone on the shelf. "You can start by calling your husband. I'm sure that will shock the hell out of him," she joked.

Brandy grinned. "But what do I say?"

"I don't know chile; he's your husband," Asè replied. "Just speak from your heart."

While Asè gathered her belongings, Brandy grabbed her phone and walked to the back of the salon. She dialed the number, and surprisingly, Mike had answered. When he did, her words flowed like a river.

"Hey, babe. I just wanted to call and tell you I love you and I am so sorry for the way I've been acting these past few months."

Mike was so happy to hear from her, they talked for ten minutes straight. Then, when he asked about the old lady, she said, "Hold on honey, let me run and go get her." But when Brandy opened the door, Asè was gone. Appalled, she sprinted to the front and peeped outside the door to see if she was waiting in the plaza somewhere. "I don't see her, babe," she said disappointedly.

Stepping back inside, Brandy walked over to the chair the old woman had sat in and saw five, one hundred dollar bills rolled together. "Babe!" Brandy shouted. "She left me enough money to pay for the rest of this month's mortgage."

Placing the phone on her shoulder, she unfolded the bills and saw a small sticky note on the last one, which read:

REMEMBER,
Chasing money doesn't bring wealth.
Serving people (joyfully) does.

Brandy smiled from ear to ear with overwhelming joy.

ALMOST A MONTH HAD GONE BY SINCE HER LAST conversation with the mysterious old woman, and things were finally looking up for Brandy. Her relationship with her husband and daughter was better than ever. And her salon was growing again, which allowed her to catch up on her house payments. But the luxurious dream home she had worked so hard to keep suddenly felt like a nightmare.

A thirteen-year-old boy was recently gunned down in their neighborhood by a white officer who had mistaken his water gun for a real one. Her husband Mike held up signs all week long in protest, which rubbed many of the residents the wrong way, inciting odd stares, accusations, and sometimes threats. The Lawson's were one of only three black families in the neighborhood. And Brandy feared for their safety every time they left the house.

So, on a Friday evening after work, Brandy and Sharina rode with Mike to check out some new homes. But the places were all in Liberty Heights, and Brandy refused to live in the same area she came from. Too many black folk in the same vicinity always leads to violence, she claimed.

Before they headed back home, Mike needed to clean out the rental property he just put his sister-in-law out of for his upcoming tenant. Turning down Gervais street to pull into the driveway, their daughter Sharina shouts, "Oh my God. Is that Corey?"

When the family got out of the car and looked across the street, they saw Officer Ricky Wallace and his son Corey guiding a large couch out of a U-Haul truck. Sharina ran over to their yard and onto the porch to greet Corey as they transported the sofa inside.

Mike walked his pregnant wife to the driveway, where they were greeted by Ricky's wife, Linda, who came out to grab something from the car. "Brandy and Mike?" She shouted perplexedly. "What are y'all doing out here?"

Brandy squinted her eyes, almost not recognizing who Linda was, as this was the first time she had ever seen her without a wig on. "We were about to ask you the same thing," Brandy said.

"Yeah," Mike interjected. "Who's moving in?"

As Linda was about to answer, the men came back outside on their last breath. "We are," Ricky answered from the porch, still gasping for air.

Mike's eyes grew wide of shock as Ricky walked over to shake his hand. After a brief small talk amongst the two couples, Mike glanced around the neighborhood, then turned to Ricky. "So, you left the good life in Lexington to live over here?" He kidded.

"Well, I don't know about the good life," Ricky said. "But yeah, I left. And I'm so glad to be back home … in Liberty Heights."

Mike stepped back lightly in disbelief. "Hold on. Are you the same Ricky Wallace I went to school with? The one who said that Liberty Heights is a dump. And so are the people in it."

"C'mon, man." Ricky laughed. "That was high school. We're grown now."

"Ricky! You told me this like five years ago … the same year you moved away from here."

Linda laughed, staring at Mike as if she knew something he didn't.

"Yeah, I know, man," Ricky said. "But things have changed. I have changed. And I want to help my community."

"Help 'em do what," Mike asked. "You planning on joining the police force out here or something?"

"Oh no," said Ricky. "I'm not joining any more organizations dedicated to killing off our people. I quit the force in Lexington. And I'm about to start my own security squad here in Liberty Heights."

Mike's jaw was on the floor. And so was Brandy's. They had known Ricky since they were kids and never had he spoke in such a revolutionary tone before. Linda, seeing the stunned look on both of their faces, tapped Brandy on the shoulder and said, "He had an encounter with Asè girl."

"Ohhhhh," Brandy said. "Now, I get it."

Looking at his wife, Mike asked, "Is that the angel lady

baby?" She nodded.

"Oh, ok." Mike raised his hands, finally understanding Ricky's transformation. "Well, why y'all ain't say that in the first place, man."

Ricky looked confused. "Hold on. You know Asè too?"

"I don't know her personally," Mike said. "But, my wife does."

Ricky turned to Brandy. "For real?"

She nodded. "Mm-hmm. That lady saved my life."

Ricky smiled, knowing exactly what she meant.

The men grabbed their women's hands and leaned against Ricky's car. Behind them were Corey and Sharina sitting on the edge of the U-Haul flirting with each other. Sharina, who was wearing her natural hair out, looked incredibly gorgeous and had Corey's full attention. As Sharina found comfort in Corey's arms, Kevin and Tina Smalls drove by, waving at his parents and the Lawson's. Zaza, who was sitting in the back seat, did a double-take at Sharina and Corey's intimate posture.

"So," Brandy looked over at Ricky, "How did you meet Asè?"

"It's a long story," he answered after a lengthy pause. "But a few weeks ago, I witnessed my partner shoot an unarmed black boy dead right in front of my eyes ... and I ... well, I just couldn't take it anymore. But when I tried to call it in, he asked me to lie and say it was self-defense. And when I got to the station, my lieutenant asked me to do the same thing. No one wanted me to confess. They said if I did, I would lose my job."

"I didn't know what to do. I mean, I knew what I saw was wrong, but I had been on the force for almost 20 years, ya know? And I didn't want to start a new career. So, I went to the boxing gym to let off some steam, and I saw an old woman in the ring giving lessons."

Everyone laughed out loud, trying to picture Asè with boxing gloves on.

"Yeah, seeing that old lady box blew me away too." Ricky laughed. "After her lesson, though, she came over to introduce herself, and we chatted for like two hours. She taught me the history of the police force and how it was created during slavery to keep black folks from freedom." Then he grinned and said, "When I told her that times have changed and that now we can change the system from within … she said something that I will never forget."

"What?" Mike asked.

She said, "You can't overcome oppression by integrating into the same system oppressing you." Everyone's head jerked back, astounded by the old woman's revelation. "Anyways," Ricky said, "by the end of that conversation, I wanted nothing else to do with the police force. At least not theirs. So I quit. And now I'm going to build my own."

"But why out here?" Brandy asked.

"Why not?" Ricky asked. "This is where we come from. And it's the only black-owned town left here in Richland County. So, if we don't protect it, then who will?"

Brandy nodded skeptically. "Well, how is the crime rate

out here … Is it safe?"

Ricky cut his teeth. "Of course. This is Beacon Hill."

"Yeah Brandy," Linda interrupted. "This is one of the safest neighborhoods in Liberty Heights. That's why we moved here. Plus, all of the community leaders live here too."

"Look," Linda said, pointing to a red house across the street. "That's Pastor Small's house." Then pointing to a blue house down the road, she said, "Jamal lives there. And Ella stays in that purple house next to him." Looking over to her left, she said, "Mr. Reed stays here. And behind him is Dane." She then pointed across the street. "And that brown house behind the one y'all are parked at … that's Baba's."

"See baby, I told you ain't nothing wrong with this area," Mike said, facing Brandy. "These are our people."

Taking it all in, Brandy began to question her beliefs. *Maybe we could live out here*, she thought. *It'd be much cheaper than what we're paying now. Plus, it's closer to the job, quiet, and safe.* She then thought about her last conversation with Asè and her vision of success. *These are the perfect ingredients for a happy home*, she concluded.

Holding her husband's hand tightly, she looked up at him and said, "Yeah, you right, babe. Let's move back home."

TEN

BROTHER UMAR FLIPPED THROUGH A STACK OF receipts and glanced out at his half-empty store from the back office. "If only this food sold like crack," he murmured as he got up to grab some boxes of produce and headed onto the floor.

Umar was the owner of Eat To Live, a new health food store on the Westside of Liberty Heights, which was the first legal business he ever had in his life. He was known as "Nino" on the streets and was once the biggest dope man in the state.

How do I know? Because he was my plug back in the day and before meeting Asè, I wanted to be just like him. But then he got arrested and was sentenced to eight years upstate. He was released about a year ago and was said to be a changed man.

Umar passed between the stacked rows of glass containers filled with grains and nuts to the produce section and removed dozens of red and yellow mangoes from his box onto the trays. His new employee, Matthew, who was already behind him laying out some cabbage and broccoli, looked at his boss with something to say.

"Yo, Mr. Robinson," he called out gently. "Can I leave early tonight?" He smiled, awaiting an answer.

Without even looking his way, Umar shook his head. "No," he exclaimed while organizing the mangoes. "We gotta finish stocking this produce to make room in the back for tomorrow's shipment."

Matthew sucked his teeth and frowned. "Man, I don't know why you still order all of this produce. Don't nobody even buy this stuff."

Umar turned around, took the kufi off his head, and grilled Matthew up and down as if he was a white man that had called him the "n" word. Although Umar had converted to Islam in prison, his old reputation for knocking people out often preceded him. And Matthew was shook.

"Do you want to keep your job?"

"Yes sir," Matthew answered with his head faced down.

"Then shut up and get back to work."

Matthew nodded intensely and finished stocking the trays, as Umar put his kufi back on and walked to the stockroom. Though he was mad, he knew in his heart Matthew was right. There were only a handful of customers in the store, and four were in the meat department. The fifth was in the checkout line with a buggy full of everything except produce.

A few moments later, an unfamiliar face entered the shop carrying a brown leather duffle bag. Matthew greeted her and asked if she needed any help. The lady smiled and replied, "Yeah, where are your mangoes, young man?" Matthew pointed behind him and walked her over to the fruits.

As the woman examined the yellow mangoes, she froze like a deer in headlights. "Whoo chile. These the most expensive mangoes I've ever seen."

"Yeah, that's why they still there," Matthew laughed out loud. Until he turned around and saw his boss angrily rushing towards the customer. Matthew's face straightened with quickness, and he began walking off as Umar approached the woman.

"Hey, ma'am. I'm Umar, the owner. Can I help you with anything?"

"Yes," she replied. "Can you help me understand why these mangoes are so high?"

Umar chuckled. "Yes, ma'am. I know our produce is higher than usual right now. But my farmers upped their fees, so this is the lowest price I can charge to make a profit."

"Well, you need to get some new farmers then."

"Believe me, if I could. I would."

She patted him on the shoulder and said, "You can, son. And you will. You just have to get a little more resourceful like you were in the streets … Nino."

Umar leaned back, removing her hand from his shoulder. "Do I know you, ma'am?"

"Not in this lifetime," the old woman answered.

Umar seemed confused. Then he stared her up and down and raised his hands. "Oh, ok. I see what this is. Look. I don't know who you are, lady, but I don't have any of that money left. So tell your boss to go to hell."

"Whoa. Whoa. Relax, son," she said calmly. "I don't have a boss. And I'm not here to collect; I'm here to give."

"Give … give me what?"

"A new perspective," she answered as she placed the duffle bag in front of her. "One that just might make your store profitable again."

After a brief moment of silence and suspicion, Umar regained his composure and directed the mysterious woman to his office.

HIS OFFICE WAS EXTREMELY SMALL, NO BIGGER than a bedroom, but it felt like an Islamic museum. Hanging on the walls were rich images of prominent black Muslims and antique décors written in Arabic. On top of the cabinets by the door was a Koran and a rolled-up prayer mat. And on the corners of his desk were two wooden LED lights in the shape of a crescent moon and five-pointed star.

As he motioned for Asè to sit down on the mini-sofa next to his desk, Umar braced himself for what she had to say. Looking around, she said, "It feels like I just walked into the Middle East."

He smiled. "So, you been to Mecca before?"

"Sure have," she answered. "But that was a long time ago. Way before you was born."

Umar stared intensely at the woman, trying to figure out her age. Then he glanced at the royal African attire and jewelry she had on. "So, who are you?"

"I AM Asè. And I'm a Perceptionist."

"A what?"

She waved her hand as to say, don't worry about it. "Just someone who can see what you can't," she said.

"Well, how do you know me?" Umar asked.

"C'mon now. Everybody knows Nino." The old woman winked and smiled.

He knew that wasn't an honest answer. But it was so true that he couldn't argue. Smiling back, he said, "Nino is dead. I am brother Umar now." He readjusted his kufi for affirmation.

"Well, if that is true, then why is the dirtiest politician in the city trying to collect money from you … brother Umar?"

"You must be talking bout Jesse?"

"Your words. Not mines."

As Umar was about to reply, he caught himself in mid-thought. "Wait. How you know about me and Jesse?"

"It doesn't matter how I know, son. But I do. And I can help you break the chains that he has over you … if you let me."

Umar tapped a pen on his desk repeatedly, trying to decide if he should confess his sins to this strange woman. Then he closed his eyes, seemingly to pray, and seconds later, he exhaled.

"Ok," he said. "To make a long story short, I used to run a drug cartel back in the day. And I paid Jesse to keep the law off me. But we eventually had some disagreements over money, and he snitched on me." He shook his head. "Anyways," he said, "When I went to jail, Jesse heard I had a million stashed away. And I did . . . at first . . . but I spent most of that on lawyer fees. The rest, I kept hidden until I got out six months ago. And I used that to open up this store."

"Jesse still thinks I have that money, though," Umar continued. "So when I first opened, he kept sending different people over here asking for his cut. That's who I thought you were," he said. Asè nodded as if she didn't already know. "And I told them just like I told you," he pointed her way, "I don't have it."

"But Jesse wasn't buying it." Umar huffed. "So he, being the snake that he is, linked up with all the local grocery store owners to put me out of business. He arranged a deal for them to each pay my farmers what I was paying them alone, as an incentive to tax me higher to the point that I'm unable to profit."

Umar pointed at the box of mangoes next to the door and said, "So that's why them mangoes are so high." They both laughed.

"That Jesse is something else ain't he," she said, shaking her head. As Umar nodded, she added, "Well, believe me, son. You not the only one he has used like this. But you will certainly be the last."

Asè placed her bag on the floor and then rubbed her hands together quickly as if she was trying to start a fire. "It's time to get started," she said.

Looking like a lost puppy, Umar opened his mouth to speak, but Asè interrupted him in typical fashion. "I hate to be the bearer of what you will deem as bad news, son, but the truth of the matter is this: your store is not failing because of Jesse. It's failing because of you."

Umar scooted back in his chair. "Excuse me, ma'am?" He shouted with force. "Did you hear what I just told you?"

"I sure did, son. I heard your entire rant about Jesse using the other grocery store owners to trap you into paying a higher tax from your suppliers. But one thing I didn't hear was why you are choosing to use the same suppliers as them?"

"Because I don't have a choice," he yelled. "They are the only batch of farmers that we can get our produce from. I mean, we got some local farmers around here that we can get greens and stuff from. But as far as the exotic fruits and veggies - those come from the same network of farmers in South America. And all of the grocery stores use them. Even the big chains."

With her head slouched forward, Asè smiled and said, "So why haven't you looked towards the eastern part of the world for suppliers?"

"I don't know," he blurted out. Then he rubbed his beard and said, "I mean ... I just never saw the eastern world as an option."

"That's because you're thinking like an American, instead of African."

He scrunched at her as if it was the furthest thing from the truth. "What you mean by that?"

"We're getting there, son," the old woman said, now leaning back on the sofa. "So answer me this: Where do the Chinese folks around here get their food supply from?"

"China, I guess."

"No guessing, son. Where do *Chinese* people get *Chinese* food from?"

"Alright. China," he answered.

"Yes. And how about the Indians, who owned all the Krishna grocery stores and restaurants. Where does their supply come from?"

"India."

"Uh-huh," she replied. "And last, what about your religious group, the Arabs who own all the gas stations around here. Where does their supply come from?"

"The Middle East."

"Indeed." She clapped. "So, considering all of the above. With you being an African, why do you seek first to get your food supply from America rather than Africa?"

Brother Umar was floored. His jaw was almost touching the desk. In all his years of being the plug, he couldn't believe he never thought of the motherland as a source. As his mind raced for an answer, he soon realized why.

"Mannn," he said in astonishment. "You're right Asè. I was thinking like an American."

"Uh-huh," she grinned. "But it's not just you, chile. It's the majority of this town. But people are slowly starting to come back to themselves. And that's the key to success … returning to your roots."

"So," Umar said, with his hands stretched outward, "You know any farmers in Africa?

The old woman smiled with a twinkle in her eye. "How bout I do ya one better," she replied. "You know Ella from the Vegan Soul Bar, right?"

"Yeah."

"Well, she gets most of her fruits and veggies from farmers in West Africa. And I hear they are ten times cheaper from the motherland than here. So you can link up with her for the plug, as y'all call it."

"That's what's up," Umar shouted. "This is amazing."

Umar pounded his fist on the table with joy. New life had sprung forth in his soul. He was now hopeful and confident that he could make his store profitable despite Jesse's tactics. But then he looked over at a poster on the wall featuring a scripture from Surah 53:38, and his smile soon became a frown.

Asè peeped Umar's change of countenance and walked over to his desk. "Hey. What's wrong, son?"

Lifting his head, he gazed at her eyes with sadness. "I appreciate all your efforts to help me get my store back profitable again. I really do. But I'm afraid this is bigger than you and me. This is Allah's judgment for my sins."

"What sins?"

Umar kept quiet.

"C'mon son. What deed have you done so bad that you should still be suffering for it today?"

After a long pause, Umar hunched over his desk and spoke. "I killed another brother once … about ten years ago," he said, in agony. "I shot him while he was sitting in his car. I cried after I pulled the trigger, wishing I could take it back. But it was too late."

Asè grimaced with pain for both him and the young man he shot. "I see," she said. "Well, you mind telling me why you killed him, son?"

"Because he was stealing money from me."

After seeing the surprised look on Asè's face, Umar added, "I know it wasn't right. But I was young and money-hungry back then. And my rep meant everything to me. So I had to take him out, or else cats would think they could steal from me too."

"I understand son. You just acted according to who you used to be."

"Yeah," he said. "But his death has haunted me for years."

Umar then reached into his wallet and removed an old wrinkled picture cut out of the funeral brochure, which read: *Jeremy Tate.*

"I've been carrying this photo in my wallet for a decade now," he said, fighting back the tears. "I keep it as a reminder of my sin so that I don't return back to that life." He looked at the scripture on the wall again and then back at the photo. "When I converted to Islam in prison and was granted the mercies of Allah, I decided that whatever happens in my life moving forward, good or bad, I deserve. So the failure of my store today is nothing more than the price of my sins."

Asè shook her head and then, out of nowhere, started laughing hysterically.

Umar looked up, confused. "That wasn't a joke, ma'am. I'm serious."

"I know," she said, trying to subdue her giggles, "That's why I'm laughing."

After regaining control of herself, Asè walked over to Umar's chair and sat on the edge of his desk to face him. "Son, there is no being in the sky, judging you for your wrongs. That's a fairytale."

"Hold up. I thought you said you went to Mecca before."

"I did," Asè answered. "But I wasn't there for religion; I was there on business."

"Aye. Well, you may not believe in a higher power, but I do," Umar said. "And I know that he is real."

"You're right son. I don't believe in a higher power. I *know* there is a higher power. But there is no separation between us and it. We are that higher power. So, the judgment that you think is coming from without is actually coming from within."

"You see, son," she elaborated, "we are all governed by universal laws. And one of those laws is that whatever you accept as truth in the subconscious of your mind—that is what you will experience in the circumstances of your life. So, it's not Allah who is punishing you. It's *you* punishing you."

As Umar was trying to decide whether he agreed with her or not, Asè placed her hand on his shoulder and said, "Never allow your past to keep your future hostage. Learn from your mistakes, but don't be a slave to them."

After her speech, the two sat still, drifting off into the distance of their minds. Asè's eyes were fixed upon the wall as if she was watching a movie. But by the terror that birthed on her face, it didn't seem like a pleasant experience. Moments later, as she was snapping out of whatever she was seeing, Umar finally responded …

"You know," he said with his finger on his chin. "You might be right Asè. I mean, all this time, I've been thinking Allah was using Jesse to punish me. But in reality, I just felt so guilty about my past that maybe I believed it was somehow righteous to allow Jesse to screw me over like this. Since it's the opposite of how I would have handled things in the past."

Asè happily smiled. "Now you see," she pointed to her right eye, "That whatever you believe is what you will receive —whether it's pleasurable or not."

As Umar was nodding at such a surreal revelation, Asè looked him in the eye and added, "You are the master of your reality, son." Then out of nowhere, she leaped up from his desk like a spring chicken. "So ward off those crutches of your past and walk boldly into your future."

Umar stood up tall in full confidence, grinning like a kid in the candy store. He gave the lady a warm hug that was so long Asè had to command him to let her go. She then grabbed her duffle bag, and Umar walked her out of the store.

As she paced through the parking lot toward the bus stop, she looked back at him and said, "The next time I visit, them mangoes better be cheaper."

Umar laughed out loud. Then walked back inside his store, a new man.

ELEVEN

"HEY, DANE!"

A warm shout echoed from the counter of The Shea Shack' as I walked inside. The Shea Shack is a natural skincare and gift shop at the very end of the Liberty Heights Plaza. It had just re-opened after being closed for the last two years and is already the premier place to go in the city for natural goods. But people don't just come for the products. They also come to get the latest gossip, as the owner Mrs. O'Neal, knew everything about everyone.

"Hey, Mrs. O'Neal! How you been?"

"Oh, I'm good, darling," she answered. "Glad to be back in business."

"Shoot … me too," I said. "I hated having to go all the way to Walmart for my shea butter. That place is a jungle."

She laughed and said, thanks. Then, all of a sudden, the latest gossip struck her mind. "Aye D. You heard about that no good dog, Councilman Jesse?"

"Nah," I said. "What happened?"

"Chile," she motioned for me to come closer as she rested her elbows on the counter, anxious to spill the tea. "How bout his wife caught him having an affair with her sister and tried to kill 'em both, but they got away." She shook her head.

"Word?"

"Yeah, man. Crazy, ain't it?" As I nodded, she said, "But listen to this, Dane. So since she couldn't catch 'em, she called the police and told them about all of the scandals he was involved in over the past ten years … and she had receipts for everything, honey."

"Dang," I said, stepping back. "When this happened?"

"Last night," she answered. "But the police ain't find Jesse until this morning. So it should be on the news in a little while." She pointed to the TV.

"How did you find this out so fast, Mrs. O'Neal?"

"Oh, I got *eyes* everywhere, baby."

I smiled. "You sound like somebody I know."

"Who?" she asked. "Your friend, Asè?"

My head turned with the quickness. "You know, Asè?"

She stood up and placed her hand on her hips. "C'mon now. You know everybody knows Asè."

"Yeah, you right. She has become quite famous around here," I said. "But how do you know her, though?"

"Well, let's just say that if it wasn't for her, I would still be closed."

I giggled and said, "So the Perceptionist set you straight, huh?"

"Yep," Mrs. O'Neal replied. "And now that I see clearly, I ain't never going out of business again."

"Have you seen her lately?" I asked.

"Yeah. I saw her this morning," she answered. "She walked past the front door waving about ten minutes before you walked in. You can probably catch her if you hurry."

"Ight, cool." I placed my usual shea butter soaps and tea tree essential oils on the counter for her to ring up, then headed towards the exit.

On my way out, I saw a poster near the door with a rose growing from the concrete on it that read, "There are seeds of greatness planted in everyone that if nurtured with discernment, can rise above anything." I smiled, happy to see my friend's words become immortalized.

Looking back at Mrs. O'Neal, I asked, "Which way was she walking … do you remember?"

She pointed to her left. "Toward Baba's."

I REALLY WANTED TO SEE ASÈ, BUT I WAS ALSO mad hungry, so I stopped by Willie's to grab me something to eat. Willie's was the only black-owned seafood joint left in town. It was run by Willie's son, Keith, who was a master chef, and a good friend. Though I no longer ate seafood, I loved their vegetarian selection and came to get my usual okra and sweet potato stew.

Stepping inside Willie's during lunchtime always gave

me the most diverse view of black people in the city. From blue-collar workers to professionals, young folks to old heads, upper class to have nots, and singles to couples; it was packed. As I made it to the front to place my order, Keith dapped me up and pointed to the right, next to the bathroom hall. I ducked my head to miss the sun blocking the view and saw Asè sitting at a table by herself.

She winked at me out the corner of her eye and raised her two fingers back and forth for me to come over. "Asè!" I hollered as I made my way to her table.

"Hey, son." She stood and embraced me with a warm hug. "You know, I thought I'd find you here."

I laughed out loud at the irony of her always seeming to find me in places like this. After all, I planned to look for her after I ate, and here she is, assuming she'd see me here. "I bet you did," I said sarcastically.

The waiter soon brought our food out, and we began grubbing. As we ate and drank, we talked about my family and the new movie project I was working on. She was happy to hear that I decided to collaborate with another black writer, but not so impressed with the content matter I chose to write about.

"I don't think leaving people behind is the message you want to send," she said.

"Huh?" I replied with a startled expression. "But you the one who taught me this though … you know, about letting go of people who hold you back."

"Letting go is one thing," she said, "but abandoning

someone is another." She pointed outside. "You see, just like those trees, we're all connected. So, when one of us is neglected, we all suffer from their decay."

I had no idea what she meant. After all that teaching she gave me back in the day about letting go of friends that weren't on the same frequency as me, this sounded like a complete contradiction. Noticing my frustration Asè motioned towards my plate, with the straightest face I'd ever seen her make. "Finish your food," she said. "We have somewhere to go."

Confused and curious at the same time, I took a couple more scoops of my stew, gulped down my lemonade, and was done. I left a tip on the counter for the waiter and followed Asè as she placed her bag around her shoulder and headed for my car. "So, where we going, Asè?" I asked, pressing the unlock button on my remote.

"Harden Street," she said. "By the old King Park."

𓂀

ASÈ DIDN'T SAY ONE WORD ON THE RIDE OVER. I wondered what was on her mind as she laid stretched out towards the back seat with her eyes closed. She seemed to be in the midst of some horrific nightmare, grimacing at every turn. But as we arrived, her trauma immediately ceased. Without even lifting her head, she smiled and said, "Park around back towards the trees."

Following her directions, I headed toward the back by the

oak trees, about thirty yards away from where we first met. The gym was still closed, but the lot had been cleaned up by the city and was often used for parking during college game nights and events. So it was much more frequented than it was back in the day. Yet, the spirit of abandonment still lingered.

As I pulled up to the brick wall of the back of the gym, Asè told me to park. She looked out of the window as if she was searching for someone and then looked back at me without speaking. Then she opened the door and began walking eastward, motioning her hand for me to follow. Watching her peak around the corner, I became a little nervous.

Asè stood against the edge of the brick wall, staring at a parked silver Chevy with the windows rolled down. When I approached her at the corner, I was stunned by what I overheard from the car. Beneath the noise of local street chatter, and cars passing to and fro, was a soft familiar cry.

The same tears that flowed down my cheeks in this very same spot ten years ago were now coming from another's. The moment was so surreal it gave me goosebumps.

As Asè walked over towards the car, I waited in the background, hidden from plain sight. Knocking on the window, I saw a young man's head jerk up and then reach for his gun. But as I took a quick step in their direction, Asè disarmed the young man with her words alone.

"Do I look like I'm here to rob you?" As the young man grinned, she added, "And if I was, I'm sure you don't need a gun to take an old woman like me." She moved her fist up back and forth in a boxing stance. The young man grinned even harder, wiping the tears from his eyes.

Watching the two exchange words felt like I was stepping into my past. I remembered Asè approaching my car in a similar fashion and me having that same response. I had no idea that night would forever change my life, and I wondered if the young man would have a similar transformation.

"Yo, who are you, lady" he asked suspiciously. "And what are you doing out here?"

"I AM Asè," she answered. "And I came here to see you."

"See me?" The young man pointed at his chest. "For what? Are you the police, lady?" He looked around his car to see if anyone else was around. I quietly stepped back to make sure he didn't spot me.

"Chile, please," Asè said, waving her hand. "But you would be an easy arrest if I was, considering the unregistered pistol you carrying and the weed you got back there in the trunk."

He gave her the same look that I did years ago. "Hold up. How did you know all that?"

She shrugged her shoulders. "I've been watching you, son," she took a step forward, "and from what I see, you're heading down the wrong path."

"Oh, really?" He looked at her sideways, mean-mugging. "And what path is that?"

"The path of destruction. Just like your father."

The young man's face softened, and his eyes grew wide. "You knew my dad?"

"No," she answered. "But I heard what happened to him. And I don't want the same to happen to you, JR."

The young man flinched. And so did I.

My best friend Jeremy, who died over a decade ago, had left behind a nine-year-old son who went by the same name. I used to visit and send money to his mother, Tameka when he was younger. But after my career took off, I lost touch with them to stay away from the streets. Jeremy's entire family was in the dope game, and I wanted no parts. So I hadn't seen JR since he was about thirteen. *Could this be him?*

"Alright, now this is getting weird," the young man replied while covertly reaching for his pistol. "How do you know me, lady?" he demanded.

"C'mon now, everyone knows you around here, son," she answered cleverly. "Now, if you'll put your gun down and invite me in for a seat next to you, then we can get started."

JR kept his hand right where it was. "Get started at what?" he asked.

"We need to start perceiving some things about your life," she answered. "We need to check out your visions and develop some discernment." After receiving no response, the old woman asked, "So can we continue this convo inside, or you gon keep an old lady out here in the cold?"

I chuckled, feeling like I was in a time machine. *She had spoken those same words to me.* And just like I did so many years ago, the young man was confused as hell on how to respond.

Yet, his curiosity allowed her to come inside. *But is this really Jeremy's son?*

JR watched the old woman like a hawk as she walked around his car towards the passenger side. "What's in the bag?" he asked, as she sat down comfortably on his plush leather seats.

"My life's work," she answered.

"And what's that?"

Asè glanced in the rear-view mirror at me with a sly smile, then turned to JR and said, "I'm a Perceptionist. I perceive things about life that other people miss. Things that produce change but are hidden behind obstacles." The old woman motioned toward the full moon behind the trees. "I see conditions and circumstances with full discernment. And that's all most people lack—is discernment—seeing the truth of a matter. So I hold the mirror up for 'em … and it empowers them to pivot, gain clarity, and transform their lives for the better."

After a brief moment of silence, JR reached in the backseat for some herbal fruit juices. One he kept for himself and the other he handed to Asè. "You want one?" he asked.

She nodded. "Sure. Thanks, son."

For a few minutes, the two sat quietly, peering off into the stars covering the sky. The irony of a street dude drinking a plant-based juice brand was interesting to me. Curious to know more about the young man, I slowly crept closer to hear their conversation, but still slightly hidden behind the shadows.

After finishing her juice, Asè leaned over towards the young man and said, "So … you just lost your best friend, huh?"

His head cocked back. "How did you know that?"

She shrugged her shoulders. "Word travels fast around here, son."

JR folded his lips and turned his head. "Well, if you already know the answer, then why you asking me?"

You sho' got a lotta anger in you man, I chuckled. *But, I know exactly how you feel. She made me mad as hell too with all 'em questions.*

The old woman smirked and said, "Relax, son. Don't get aggravated with ol' Asè." She placed her hand on top of the young man's knee and added, "I'm just here to help … ok?"

Accepting his nod, Asè continued. "I want you to know that I am truly sorry for your loss. But if you don't make some major changes in your life, you will end up just like Chris."

JR swallowed his juice and then slammed the bottle in his cup holder. "So you came out here to tell me I'm going to die, lady?"

I asked her that very same question.

"Those are your words, not mines," Asè answered. "All I said was that you were heading down the path that your friend went on—leaving your body before completing your mission. I ain't say nothing about dying."

JR looked confused. "What's the difference … ain't they the same thing?"

"No, son." She shook her head. "Death is impossible.

Once life is manifested, it can never die. The spirit is eternal and lives through many lifetimes. And so does the flesh. It gets buried in the ground, decomposes, and becomes a part of nature."

"Wow!" JR said. "How you know all of this old lady?"

"Ohhhh ... Let's just say I've been around the block a few times."

He knew what she meant, but he wasn't sure if he believed her. "So you saying Chris ain't dead ... he just became a part of nature?" He asked in a sarcastic tone.

"Not yet, son," she answered. "It's too soon. But over time, he will ... his flesh, that is."

JR stroked his beard, pondering for a moment. "What about his spirit then?" he asked. Where is that at?"

"In another realm," she answered. "But, his energy is still projected right here."

The old woman's confidence in Chris's whereabouts made JR curious. But as he opened his mouth to speak, Asè interrupted. "And he's safe where he's at. So you don't have to go out there and defend him."

A long deep sigh blew from the young man's breath. "But it's my fault he's gone, though. If it wasn't for me, he would still be here."

Asè shook her head. "Why you say that, son?"

"It's a long story."

"Well, I ain't got nothing but time, son ... so shoot."

"Ok," he surrendered. "Because we got into a shootout at this club ... against some fuck boys I had beef with since back in high school … and I made it out, and Chris didn't."

"Do you think that was a coincidence?" she asked. The young man looked puzzled and offended. "I mean for you to have beef with some guys for so many years, do you think it's a coincidence that they killed him and not you … that you lived and he didn't?"

"It don't matter what I think. Either way, he's gone."

Asè peered into the young man's eyes and gently touched his shoulder. "I'm sorry how things went down that night, son. I truly am." Then, removing her hand, she said, "But if your past doesn't matter to ya, then neither does your future."

The old woman's response made the young man turn red. "What you mean by that?"

"Oh nothing," Asè said with a bogus innocence. "I was just agreeing with you, that's all."

JR stared Asè down with fury. She had trapped him with his own words, just as she had done with me, many times over. Watching the scene from the background, I almost blew my cover with laughter.

"Look," he shouted. "I know my life is a mess. But it ain't nothing I can do about it, ok? So just leave me alone, lady."

"If I wanted to leave you alone, I wouldn't have come to see you tonight. But you betta learn to respect your elders before you get hurt, son." Looking at the old woman's calm yet assertive demeanor, the young man became silent. "Anyways," she said, "the statement you made about your life is only half true."

"What you talking bout?" he asked.

"Well, you said that your life is a mess," Asè replied. "That is true. And it's getting messier by the day. But," she raised her finger, "the part about you not being able to do anything about it—that's false, son. All messes can be cleaned up."

I saw the wheels spinning in the young man's head from the rearview mirror. He looked offended and hopeful at the same time. Asè had him right where she wanted.

"Son," Asè said in the sweetest tone. "What would you say if I told you that Chris was going to end up dead that night regardless of going to the club, but as a result of his death, you are exactly where you need to be, to create the life you desire to live?"

Asè turned to the side view mirror and gave me a wink. I grinned as I remembered her asking me almost that very same question, in this very same spot.

"I would say how you know that?" the young man asked.

"Because I've been watching Chris too, and his criminal ways had caught up with him," she answered. "So now that his choices have led him to an early grave, you are free to travel a different path. One that ain't so … messy."

The young man deliberated over her comments. "I wouldn't even know what a clean life looks like," he thought out loud. "The streets are all I know."

Asè smiled at the young man, finally letting down his guard. "Well, how about this. If you could do or be anything you wanted to be, what would what that be, son?"

"Well," he thought, "when I was a kid, I used to wanna be like an herbalist or something dealing with nature. I always had a fascination with plants and herbs and making things with them. I know this might sound crazy, but I even used to talk to plants, and they would talk back."

Asè grinned. "No, that don't sound crazy at all. That's quite normal in our culture. Many of your ancestors had the same ability you have. They were known as shamans, medicine men, and root doctors."

"Yeah … root doctors," JR said. "That's what my grandma 'dem used to call me. But they said it like it was evil or something. My dad felt the same. Anytime he would see me talking to plants in the yard at mama house, he would say, 'Cut that stuff out, boy. You gon mess around and put roots on us.' So after he passed, I just stopped dealing with plants altogether." Then he caught himself. "Well, except for weed."

They both laughed.

"Yeah, it's unfortunate," Asè replied. "But many of our people think like this. We are so far removed from our culture that we now see what's good for us as evil and what's bad for us as good." She looked down, shaking her head, then picked it right back up. "Listen, son. There is nothing evil about nature. We are nature, and she is us. And you have a gift—a natural ability to work with her. So never again, let anyone stop you from going after what's in your heart to do."

JR nodded with his eyes fixed on her mouth as his mind processed the words that just came out of it. After a long stare, he said, "So you really think I can be an herbalist?"

"You already are, son. That's why you're so good at growing and selling weed," she said teasingly. "You just need to leave these streets alone and go legit."

"But what if it doesn't work out?" he asked. "Right now, I'm the top dog. But these young niggas out here just itching for a chance to take my spot. So if I try this herbalism stuff out and it doesn't work …"

"Focus on winning, son, not losing," Asè butted in. "Whatever you place focus on becomes your reality."

JR took a moment to let her proverb sink in, and then asked, "So, how do I go about becoming legit? I don't even know anyone who runs their own business."

"Yes, you do, son. You remember your pop's best friend, Dane?"

I knew it. That's him. I pumped my fist.

"Yeah," JR answered. "Wait. You know him too?"

"Mm-hm. He's a good friend of mines. And y'all have quite a lot in common."

"Man, I haven't seen him in years … Since I was like in middle school," he said. "My mama said he used to send us money after my dad died. But then he blew up and became Hollywood and forgot about us."

From the shadows, I put my head down in shame. *I didn't mean to abandon y'all, man. I was just doing what I felt was best for my success.*

"Well," the old woman said, "there are two sides to every story. So maybe you can hear his one day. He's back in town and hangs out at Baba's a lot … if you're ever looking for him."

"In the meantime," she continued, "I want you to remember this. Everything you need to succeed lives within you. And all of the opportunities you seek live around you. You just have to grow enough to see them."

"I don't get this one, Asè … the part about having to grow to see?"

"Well, just like plants," she pointed to the left at the community garden, "Life is all about growth. So, the more you water your soul with love, knowledge, and people who uplift you, the more you will notice opportunities in alignment with your calling."

"Sheesh," he said with his eyes widened. "Ok, I get it now!"

"Of course you do; you're an herbalist!" she replied. Patting him on the back, she concluded, "I just came to remind you of who you are."

JR smiled, showcasing his teeth for the first time. Asè returned a similar smile and then reached for her bag on the floor. "Well, I have to go now. But I have a few gifts for you to help you grow." Holding her hand inside the bag, she asked, "Do you read?"

"Yeah, sometimes."

"Well, add these to your collection," she said, as she pulled out three paperback books to hand to him. I moved closer to see if any of them were the ones she had given to me, but they weren't. They were handpicked just for him. *Imhotep*, *The Man Who Talks With The Flowers*, and *Of Water and the Spirit.*

JR thanked Asè for the books as she exited his car. He offered to give her a lift, but she gracefully declined.

As I walked back to my ride a few minutes later, I felt a little down about not being there for my best friend's son. But I was beyond grateful that Asè had entered into his life at just the right time as she had done for me. Then, looking around at the now emptiness of the parking lot, I suddenly understood why I came here a decade ago. It was abandoned, just like I was. And that same vibration had brought JR here.

When I turned around to open my car door, Asè wasn't on the other side. So I walked back to the brick wall to see if she had gone back to JR, but she wasn't there either. I searched the entire parking lot, but she was nowhere to be found. After wracking my brain trying to figure out where she went, I decided to just go home. I figured maybe she had somewhere else to be and that I would run into her again somewhere like always.

It wasn't until the weekend when I discovered that the woman responsible for changing my life was gone, and this time for good.

TWELVE

MY DOORBELL RUNG AT 7:57 A.M. ON THE FIRST Friday of August. I was upstairs in my office working on a new script, so I didn't bother to get up. It's probably the amazon man dropping something off, I figured. My wife, who was in the kitchen making breakfast, thought the same. But when she heard the dog barking at someone on the porch, she decided to open the door.

Peaking outside, she saw no one there. "Who you barking at Badu?" she asked. The dog stood up, patted her legs with joy, and then ran inside the house to play with the kids. "I'll be right back," Lashonda said, looking back at the kids. She walked down the porch and into the yard to look around, but no one was in sight.

"Badu must've hit the doorbell," she said to herself. But on her way back up the steps, she noticed a brown leather duffle bag leaning against the porch wall. She looked around one more time just in case and then immediately ran inside the house.

I heard three hard pounds on my office door before Lashonda frantically entered in. "Hey babe," she said, gasping for air, "I'm sorry to bother you … but I just saw Asè's bag outside."

I jumped out of my seat. "For real? Where?"

"On the porch," she answered. "It was just leaning up against the wall by the bench. I looked around to see if anyone was there, but I ain't see nobody."

"Are you sure it was hers?" I asked.

"Yeah, go down and see."

I saved my work and ran downstairs. As soon as I saw the bag, I knew it was hers. Nobody had a bag like this but her. But what was it doing here on my porch? Where was Asè? Did she leave it here on purpose, or was she snatched up by someone on her way to see me?

After running through multiple scenarios in my head, I finally kneeled to pick up the bag. Holding it up, I turned it over and over, searching for a sign but found none. I wanted to open it, but I didn't want to invade her privacy. So I called the only person in town who would know what to do.

"Peace. Love. And Black Power. This is Baba," the old man answered.

"Yo, Baba, this is Dane."

"DC!" he exclaimed. "What's happening, my man?"

"Man, I hate to bother you this early, but …"

"Ahhh, cut it out," Baba said. "You ain't bothering me. What's up?"

"Baba, you won't believe this. I just found Asè's bag on

my porch, but she ain't nowhere in sight."

"Really?" he asked. "Are you sure it's hers?"

"C'mon, man, I wouldn't be calling you if I wasn't."

"Yeah, that's true young blood," he replied. "So, when was the last time you saw her?"

"I was with her like three nights ago near BC," I replied. "Ain't heard from her since, though."

After a few moments of silence, he responded. "Well, did you take a look and see what's inside?"

"Nah. I thought about it, but it felt like I would be committing a sin or something."

Baba laughed out loud. "Well, bring the bag down here to the store. We can figure it out together before the rest of the plaza opens up."

"Ight. I'll be there in a minute."

I told Lashonda where I was headed, then quickly ran upstairs, took off my basketball shorts and slippers, and threw on some jeans and Nikes. I washed my face, brushed my grill, ran back downstairs, told the kids bye, grabbed the bag, and was in the car in less than ten minutes.

I PULLED INTO THE PARKING LOT AND PARKED next to Baba's 93' Buick. He was right. All of the businesses still had 'closed' signs on the door. Everyone, except his. As I walked past the other stores, I saw Mrs. O'Neal peeking through the windows of The Shea Shack, looking down at the bag in my hand. I could tell she recognized it, so I knew it was only a matter of time before the gossip queen would spread the word.

Entering the bookstore, I didn't see Baba behind the counter, so I walked over to the café. As he spoke with his employees by the register, he gave me a nod and motioned for me to come over. Baba stared down at the bag, then, looking back up at me, he said, "It seems so weird seeing that bag in someone else hands."

"Yeah," his manager Derek said. "I ain't never seen Asè without that bag. Something has got to be wrong."

"That's the same thing I thought when I saw it on my porch."

Baba reached his hand out. "Let me hold it, son."

After I gave him the bag, he turned it over and over, looking for clues, it seemed, and then walked over to the nearest table and sat it on top. As he rubbed his hand over the bag one more time, he closed his eyes as if he was praying over it. Then suddenly, he looked up facing me and said, "Maybe she left you this bag on purpose, Dane."

"Why would she do that?"

"I don't know," he said. "But I've been knowing Asè for quite a while. Longer than most. And nothing she does is without reason."

As I pondered over why Asè would leave me the bag, I saw one of Baba's two employees behind the café counter pointing at something outside. Looking out the glass windows, I saw Mrs. O'Neal, Ella, Jamal, my aunt Brandy and about six others headed our way, with straight and concerned faces.

Upon entering the café, everyone's eyes immediately turned towards the table. "Hey, what's going on, fellas?" Ella asked.

Before we could respond, Mrs. O'Neal bluntly added, "Yeah, what's Asè's bag doing here?"

Baba pointed at the bag and said, "Dane found it on his porch this morning and brought it here."

Watching everyone's eyes suspiciously turn to me, I declared, "Yeah, it was crazy. Somebody rang the doorbell, and my wife checked it and saw Asè's bag laying up against the porch bench." Looking at Ella, I said, "I ain't know what to do, so I called Baba."

"Well," Brandy said, "When was the last time you seen her?"

"About 3 days ago."

Brandy turned her head slightly and rubbed her fingers through her hair. I could see the wheels turning in her head. "That's the last time I saw her too." Then she placed her hands on her hips and continued. "She came by the shop real late before I closed up. We had finished a convo from the other week. Then she gave me one of her parables," Brandy laughed, "and left."

"I saw Asè on Tuesday as well," Ella interrupted. She placed her hand on the table next to the bag and said, "She was having lunch with some young guy at the restaurant. When I brought their plates over, she bragged to him about me and my food. Later, as they were leaving, she looked back and gave me a wink," Ella smiled, "Then they headed out."

"Man, this is crazy," Jamal chimed in. " I saw her on Tuesday too. "She was working at the center with youth as usual ... schooling them on life and stuff." Then he breathed in a deep sigh. "Before she left for the day, she gave me a big hug, bigger than normal, and said 'our community,' referring to the center, 'extends much further than Columbia.' When I asked her what she meant, she told me, 'You'll see' and walked off."

"Humph," Mrs. O'Neal muttered. "Well, I guess I'm the only one she didn't see on Tuesday."

"Hell, it wasn't no need for her to come see you," Baba replied. "You know more about us than she did."

Everyone broke out in laughter.

"Ha-ha," Mrs. O'Neal retorted. "I just like to know what's going on round here, that's all."

"Well, you are definitely the expert at that," Brandy teased. "I didn't even know about the bag until you called the shop a few minutes ago."

"Yeah, me neither," Ella replied.

Jamal and the rest of the crowd said the same.

As I looked up, amid all the laughter, I noticed that the crowd had gotten larger. It was now over twenty people around the table behind us, with more people walking inside. And from what I could tell, most of them didn't even work in the plaza. So Mrs. O'Neal's word was indeed spreading.

Derek must've noticed the crowd because he had started bringing out coffee and teas to the tables. We were all regulars, so he knew what we liked. Once the drinks made it to us, me and Baba grabbed some seats around Asè's bag, and everyone else followed suit.

"Asè saved my life last week," Mr. Woods, the owner of the cleaner's down the street, spoke out to everyone. "If I hadn't met her, I wouldn't be here right now." We all looked back at him. "Is she ok?" he asked, looking in my direction.

"I don't know, sir." I shrugged my shoulders. "It's hard to tell right now. None of us have seen her in a few days. And all we have left of her is this bag."

Immediately, everyone began staring at the duffle bag in the center of the room that was quickly becoming famous. Then the door opened, shifting our attention to several more faces entering the café, including Mr. Reed, Pastor Smalls, and his wife Tina. Mr. Reed grabbed a chair from the window and pulled up next to me. "I heard about the bag?" he said. "Any updates yet?"

I shook my head. "Nope."

Derek started pouring more coffee and tea for the newcomers. At Baba's command, the two cashiers began distributing big plates of bagels on all the tables. As we ate and drank in silence, more people strolled in like every ten minutes. I saw Willie, Keith, Gilbert and Wanda Suell, Tameka and JR, Dr. Hemmit, Uncle Mike, and the Wallace's. And these were just the people that I knew.

Although the place was now packed, it was as quiet as a mouse. All you could hear were cups hitting the table and chairs moving. Occasionally, you would hear a greeting, but even that was done in a whisper. It was beginning to feel like a funeral. And I couldn't take it anymore.

"Hey, what's up, everybody?" I shouted in a cheerful tone. "I was wondering … does anyone know where Asè lives … or sleeps at?" Everyone looked around at each other, hoping to hear that someone knew. But no one did. All I got was blank stares. "I figured that," I sighed.

"Well, maybe we're overreacting, DC," Pastor Smalls said. "I mean from what I've heard, this ain't the first time Asè has gone missing, is it?"

"No," Ella answered before I could respond, "But this is the first time she has left her bag, though. I've known Asè for over 20 years, and I ain't never seen her without that bag."

"Yeah, pastor, she always has that bag with her," I said.

Once again, everyone's attention shifted toward the bag. I hadn't touched it since I gave it to Baba. Neither did anyone else.

"Does anybody know where Asè is from?" someone yelled from the crowd.

Everyone shook their heads.

"She's gotta be from heaven," Anthony White answered. "I was doing ten-to-twenty when I met Asè. Had it not been for her, I would still be in prison today."

All heads turned toward the left window in the back. Anthony White? Prison? I had no idea. And judging by the raised eyebrows all around the room, no one else did either. Anthony was a clean-cut and clean-shaven military vet who worked at Crews as a fitness trainer. He had no tattoos, piercings, or any other trace of jail written on him; and was one of the nicest dudes you could ever meet. Word on the street was that he was dishonorably discharged from the military, but no one knew why. It looked like we were all about to learn now, though.

"I never told anyone this before," Anthony began, "but when I was in the service, I got caught smuggling dope from Asia into the states and was sent upstate. I thought my life was over and that my best years would be spent behind those walls. But one night in the joint … when I was sleeping … I heard this voice that kept calling my name. When I woke up, I saw this old lady with a glow around her, staring down at me. I was scared as hell, but her presence immediately calmed me down.

"Anyways," he said, "the lady knew who I was and all sorts of things about me. We talked for hours about life, and she helped me see things about myself I never knew before. Then she told me that she had to go, but that if I was free mentally, then I would soon be free physically."

Many heads nodded and smiled, finding familiarity in those words.

"I didn't know what she was talking about … but the next day around 3:00, the guard came to my cell and told me the warden wanted to see me. I thought I was in trouble because he was an old racist white man and was mean as hell. But when I got to his office that day, he showed me nothing but love and told me that a mutual friend came to visit him; and gave him new eyes. Then he explained that he made arrangements for me to enter into this early release program for veterans, and about six months later, I was free."

Anthony suddenly became a loss for words. He placed his hand over his mouth and stared at the ground, in deep thought about something we were all on the edge of our seats to hear. After several seconds of waiting, Pastor Smalls broke the silence. "So who let Asè out of your cell," he asked. "Did she know the guards or something?"

Anthony turned towards Pastor Smalls and smiled peculiarly at what he was about to say. "No, she let herself out," he said. "She walked straight through the bars as if she was a ghost or something. Then she waved at me goodbye, walked down the hall, and then vanished into thin air."

"Hell naw," shouted Pastor Smalls. "I don't believe that. Can't be."

"Yeah, I don't know about that one now," Mr. Reed said.

"Well, y'all can believe whatever you want," Anthony replied. "But I know what I saw."

"But, are you sure that was Asè, though?" Ella asked.

Anthony gave Kevin the poot face. "Yes!" he answered. Then he pointed towards the table and said, "She had that same bag in her hand right there."

"And when was this?" I turned towards Anthony. "That night, she came to your cell?"

"About 7 years ago," he answered. "That was right before I came back here to Liberty Heights. But I ain't seen her since … until she showed back up a few months ago."

"She changed my life too," a soft voice echoed from the crowd.

All heads flipped backward to a voice near the

bookshelves on the left sidewall. It was Ebony Hill, the women's swim team coach for Benedict University. We were around the same age but went to different high schools, so I didn't know her too well. But she was a fixture in the community due to the back to back championships she won over the last few years.

Ebony stood up. "Like Anthony," Ebony said, glancing in his direction, "I've never told anyone this before." She stopped for a beat and took a loud, deep breath. "But before I moved back home to coach, I used to be in a wheelchair."

A flood of gasps filled the room.

"Yep." She nodded. "I was hit by an 18-wheeler when I was competing overseas and broke both my legs. The doctors said I would never walk again," Ebony said, shedding a tear. "Basketball was all I ever wanted to do, so I felt like my life was over." She leaned back on the shelf, gazing into the distance as if she had an epiphany. "But then I met Asè."

I had been in town low-key for a few months, and my mom got tired of me complaining, so she forced me to go fishing with her and my dad at Lake Congaree. When we got there, we saw Asè on a boat in the middle of the waters. She had her eyes closed and moving her body in these funny motions," she laughed. "I couldn't keep my eyes off the old woman, so after she was done, we called her over to ask what she was doing."

"It turns out that she was doing Kemetic yoga and claimed that if I took on this ancient practice, that I would learn to walk again. My parents didn't believe her, and neither did I. But I ain't have nothing to lose, so I let her teach me," she said. "First, she taught me its origins, then she showed me some breathing techniques, body movements, and chants that I could use to empower myself. And I never forgot them." Ebony smiled ecstatically, looking down at her legs. "Yoga not only helped me walk again—it made me one of the best swimmers in the states."

Everyone nodded, now understanding how Ebony's renowned yoga-centered swimming techniques came about.

"Anyways," Ebony continued, "Me and Asè talked for hours that night. So, needless to say, I didn't catch any fish." As everyone laughed, Ebony motioned for silence. "Here's the kicker, though," she said. "When I strolled back to the other side of the river where my parents were, they asked me where the old lady went, and I pointed behind me. But when we looked back, she wasn't there. We spent the next half hour searching for her, but I never saw Asè again," she sighed. "Until recently."

After Ebony sat down, the room went back silent for a few short minutes. Then, without warning, everyone began talking. For over two hours, people told story after story about Asè and how she helped transform their lives for the better. My mom, Sherri Carter—who was now living with me—had crept in while Ebony was still talking and encouraged me to share how I met Asè and want she had done for me.

Baba stood up next and told us about meeting Asè when he was 14 years old and how the old woman saved him from a career in grand theft autos by sparking his interest in reading and collecting books. His teenage collection became the inventory for his bookstore. *Who knew?*

Willie stepped forward and said he was a homeless crackhead on Main Street when he first saw Asè. He used to cook seafood for pushers in exchange for dope until Asè hired him to be her chef for the Crews homeless program. Many of the older folks nodded, remembering him from back in the day. She guided him through some African rituals that took away his addiction, he told us, and the money he saved up allowed him to open up his Seafood joint.

After a while, no one had any more stories to tell. Or at least, they weren't sharing them. Looking around the café, I noticed there were now more than eighty people jammed together into this small café, with even more listening in from the bookstore. And every one of them, I was certain, had been transformed by Asè in some form or fashion.

Sitting next to Baba, Ella, and Mrs. O'Neal, as we each meditated on all the stories we had just heard, my mind began to wonder. *Who is this lady? Was she human? Was she a Goddess? Or was she just a medicine woman with oracle abilities like the ancestors I read about?*

In the middle of my thoughts, someone yelled from the crowd … "So, is somebody gon open the bag, or we gon sit here all day staring at it?"

Everyone turned toward the direction of the voice. I didn't recognize who it was, but I damn sure agreed with his question. "What you wanna do, Baba?" I asked, pointing at the bag.

"It's your call, son." He replied. "She left *you* the bag."

Nervously, I stood up and turned around to face the crowd. "So what y'all think … should I open it?"

Everyone looked around at each other, scared to blurt out the wrong answer. I could tell that many wanted to say yes, but at the same time didn't want to violate Asè's privacy. Then Mrs. O'Neal, who was sitting across from me, reached over and tapped me. "Well, I don't know about everybody else, but I think you should open it, DC."

Nodding my head, I looked around at the blank faces in the crowd and said, "Well, ight then. I guess I'll go ahead and open it."

Willie stood up, waving his finger side to side. "Ah ah ah," he said. "No guessing, son."

We all laughed out loud.

"Ok. I'm opening it."

As I grabbed the bag and turned it over towards the buttoned-straps, I could feel everyone in the room leaning in towards me. It was so quiet inside that café that you could hear our hearts beating. Tilting the bag forward, I popped open the straps and opened it halfway, but nothing came out. So I opened the bag wide and flipped it upside down on the table. Everyone leaned in once again, hoping for maybe one of Asè's gifts, to fall out. But none did.

I scratched my head and glanced at Baba, who shrugged his shoulders with disappointment. Then, interrupting our perceived failure, Mrs. O'Neal stood up and reached for the bag. "Here. Give it to me," she said.

After doing as she asked me to, Mrs. O'Neal rubbed her hand all through the inside of the bag, then looked up at me and said, "I think I feel something …"

Everyone in the room stood up from their seats.

"Word?" I shouted. "What is it?"

She pulled out a brown envelope that was tucked in the bottom of the bag. Cracking the seal and sliding the piece of paper out of it, Mrs. O'Neal saw Asè's name at the bottom.

"Look y'all. It's a note from Asè." She held it up for all to see.

"Really?" I asked. "Well, what it say?"

Before she could open her mouth, Baba interrupted. "Wait!" he said. "Give it to Dane. He should read it."

I could tell that Mrs. O'Neal didn't want to. But she knew that Baba was right, so she handed me the letter.

Baba tapped me on the chest and said, "Read it out loud, so we can all hear."

"Ight," I said. Flattening out the paper, my hands began to sweat. So I wiped them on my pants and then began to read:

To my beloved descendants,

In ancient times, on the shores of Kemit and Kush, lived a royal african tribe who led the world in commerce. They later migrated to various parts of the world to expand their territories. Most of them settled in West

Africa in modern-day Nigeria, Ghana, Sierra Leonne, and Senegambia. The rest sailed across the seas and set roots in what is now called the Americas. And each of the regions traded with each other for business.

Governing all of the tribes was a royal lineage of matriarchs, going back over 3,000 years. In 1403, the daughter of a priestess inherited spiritual leadership over all the tribes. But instead of leading her people to enlightenment, she chose to chase after riches. The young priestess created a collection of fine leather handbags and established relationships with wealthy European traders, to sell them abroad. But the whites had a hidden agenda, which eventually led to millions of her people being enslaved in both Africa and the Americas.

By the time she realized what she had done, it was too late. Her people were gone, along with her husband, and she spent the rest of her life miserably rich and lonely. But the lessons she had learned made her the wisest woman in the world.

In her old age, she pleaded to her great ancestor from which we all came, to help her redeem their bloodline from oppression. In return, she was granted with the option to be reincarnated as half-human, half-spirit with full-memory and abilities until her mission is complete. The catch was her true identity had to remain hidden and that she would suffer from post-traumatic flashbacks to keep her on point.

She agreed to the terms and was sent to the

Americas to find the remnants of her tribe, and give to them what she once lacked—discernment.

After centuries of work, her tribe has now been restored and is becoming self-sufficient again. Some have even moved back to Africa. But the vast majority remain in the Americas. The last of them reside in a small town within Columbia, SC, called Liberty Heights.

Those who have the eyes, let them see.

-Asè

In the middle of reading the letter, I realized just who we were to her. And by the end of it, I knew that I would probably never see her again. And so did everyone else in the room.

After a few minutes of silence, people began walking towards the table. Some came to read the note themselves, while others just came to grieve. After most of the crowd had left, me and Baba discussed the letter and made plans to finish what Asè had started.

In the months that followed, the community developed an interest in their African roots like never before. People were wearing dashikis, learning about their history, practicing African spirituality, and even taking trips to the motherland. Facilitating all of these needs was Pastor Kevin and Tina Smalls, who renamed their church, The African Village. Everyone goes there now, including Christians and Muslims.

After the massive rise of spirituality, came a massive rise in economics. People began pooling their resources together and forming collective businesses where everyone shares ownership and profit. From there, alliances were made to only buy from each other, which led to most of the non-black businesses, to close up shop. And the Heights is now a black mecca again.

As for the old brown leather duffle bag? Baba placed it inside a squared glass display box that he mounted on the wall in his bookstore. It has since become a historic monument for the community, and people travel near and far just to see it and hear about the legend of its owner.

When the mayor and other politicians found out about it, they could not believe that such events happened on their watch and without their assistance. So, they took to the media and called the story a myth. In response, I made a documentary film about it that featured hundreds of testimonies from locals, which became a national hit. And our local government was forced to accept the fact that the Liberty Heights community was revived by the discernment given to us from an old woman, named Asè.

THE PERCEPTIONIST

READER'S GUIDE

CHARACTER LIST

All of the character's names appear in alphabetical order.

Anthony – The clean-cut fitness trainer at Crews.

Asè – The protagonist of *The Perceptionist.* She's a West African high priestess and Orisha from the 15th century, who visits Columbia, SC to redeem the last generation of her tribe.

Baba – The owner of Baba's Books & Café. Former Black Panther and oldest living elder in the community.

Baba – The puppy that was given to Sanaa and Omari.

Brandy – Dane's aunt-in-law. Owner of She Styles Hair.

Brother Umar – Dane's former plug. Reformed Muslim. Owner of Eat to Live.

Corey – The lost teenager with jungle fever who worked at Crews for the summer. The son of Ricky and Linda Wallace.

Dane – The narrator of *The Perceptionist.* He's a street dude from Benedict Courts Projects who shares his testimony of Asè from ages twenty-two to thirty-three.

Dr. Hemmit – The money-hungry know it all doctor who owns a pharmacy in Liberty Heights. Also, the younger brother of Baba.

Ebony – The renowned women's swim coach at Benedict University.

Ella – The owner of Soul Vegan Café.

Gilbert – The self-righteous housing authority director over Benedict Courts.

JR – The son of Dane's best friend.

Jamal – The neighborhood-friendly owner of Crews Community Center.

Jesse – The name of the crooked City councilman that's helping white people gentrify the town.

Keith – The master chef behind Willie's seafood.

Lashonda – Dane's wife.

Linda – The wife of Officer Ricky.

Mariah – The young and innocent daughter of Gilbert.

Matthew – The lazy grown son of Gilbert.

Mike – Dane's uncle. A wanna-be landlord. Husband to Brandy and Sharina's stepdad.

Mr. Reed – Owner of Reed's Funeral Home. Buried Dane's father and best friend.

Mr. Woods – The owner of a Liberty Height's cleaners.

Mrs. O'Neal – The town's gossip queen and owner of The Shea Shack.

Omari – Dane's five-year-old son.

Pastor Smalls – The former pastor of Living Through The Word Ministries.

Ricky – Veteran police officer. Corey's dad.

Sanaa – Dane's seven-year-old daughter.

Sharina – An insecure college sophomore. Brandy's daughter.

Sherri – Dane's mother.

Tameka – Struggling single mother of two girls and a wild and crazy son, JR.

Tina – Pastor Small's holier-than-thou wife.

Wanda – The soft-spoken wife of Gilbert.

Willie – The owner of Willie's Seafood.

ZaZa – The beautiful, pro-black high school basketball star.

ASÈ'S PROVERBS

All of the quotes appear in chronological order.

1. In order to accomplish the work you were created to do, you have to become the person you were created to be.
2. What you focus on, grows. What you ignore, dies.
3. Your character must be in alignment with what you desire to manifest.
4. You can't change what you can't see.
5. Marriage is a mirror of your relationship with yourself.
6. In order to see God in others, you have to first see God in yourself.

7. Never put those who came before you at the end of your priorities.
8. The stronger your emotions are towards something, the likelier you will draw it to you.
9. The study of nature is the study of self.
10. The most intelligent mind you have is the one connected to your bloodline.
11. You can't truly love another until you first learn to love yourself.
12. We are all emanations of *The All*.
13. The home you desire to live in, build it. The neighbor you desire to have, be it. The food you desire to eat, grow it. The land is rich, but you have to produce what you desire to see.
14. The only power white folks have over you is the power you give them.
15. Forgive yourself for your mistakes and wrongs towards others, so you can forgive others for their mistakes and wrongs towards you.
16. Life ain't about you. It's about everybody.
17. How we do one thing is usually how we do everything.

18. Losses build bridges to wins.
19. What brings you joy, will bring you success.
20. Chasing money doesn't bring wealth; serving people does.
21. You can't overcome oppression by integrating into the same system oppressing you.
22. Never allow your past to keep your future hostage. Learn from your mistakes, but don't be a slave to them.
23. Just like those trees, we're all connected. So when one of us is neglected, we all suffer from their decay.
24. Whatever you place your focus on becomes your reality.
25. Everything you need to succeed lives within you.

BOOKS MENTIONED

All books are listed in the order they were mentioned.

CHAPTER 1:

Alex Haley. *The Autobiography of Malcolm X: As Told To Alex Haley.*

Tyrese Gibson. *How To Get Out of Your Own Way.*

Patrick McGilligan. *Oscar Micheaux: The Life of America's First Black Filmmaker.*

CHAPTER 2:

Rupert Lewis. *Marcus Garvey: Caribbean Biography Series.*

Dr. Tyrene Wright. *Booker T. Washington and Africa: The Making of A Pan-Africanist.*

Nathan McCall. *Makes Me Wanna Holler: A Young Black Man in America.*

Jeffrey Babcock Perry. *Hubert Harrison: The Voice of Harlem Radicalism.*

Margena A. Christian. *Empire: The House That John H. Johnson Built.*

Eric Thomas. *The Secret to Success.*

A.G. Gaston. *Green Power: The Successful Way of A.G. Gaston.*

Barbara Eleanor Adams. *John Henrick Clarke: Master Teacher.*

Amiri Baraka. *The Autobiography of Leroi Jones.*

CHAPTER 3:

John G. Jackson. *Christianity Before Christ.*

CHAPTER 5:

Muata Ashby. *Kemetic Diet: Ancient African Wisdom for Health of Mind, Body and Spirit.*

CHAPTER 8:

Dennis Kimbro. *Think and Grow Rich: A Black Choice.*

Reggie Whittaker. *As A Black Man Thinketh: A Guide to Self-Empowerment and Black Excellence.*

Frederick Eikerenkoetter. *Rev. Ike's Secrets For Health, Joy and Prosperity, For YOU: A Science of Living Study Guide.*

Queen Afua. *Sacred Woman: A Guide to Healing The Feminine Body, Mind, and Spirit.*

CHAPTER 11:

Jamieson B. Hurry. *Imhotep: The Egyptian God of Medicine.*

Glenn Clark. *The Man Who Talks With The Flowers: The Intimate Life Story of Dr. George Washington Carver.*

Malidoma Somè. *Of Water and the Spirit: Ritual, Magic and Initiation in the Life of an African Shaman.*

ABOUT THE AUTHOR

Mo'Reese Madu is an online entrepreneur, author, poet, and screenwriter. After working as a web designer and content marketer for several years, Mo'Reese decided to pursue his passion of storytelling. *The Perceptionist* is his debut novel, which he's currently adapting into a TV-Series. He resides in Columbia, SC with his wife and children; where he spends most of his days writing and homeschooling. To connect with Mo'Reese, please visit his blog at MoreeseMadu.com.

CPSIA information can be obtained
at www.ICGtesting.com
Printed in the USA
LVHW090456070521
686668LV00005B/9

9 781732 899377